IN THE ZONE OF CHANGES

A new millennium author makes a siren
resound in America's changing mores

IN THE ZONE OF CHANGES

ODESSA CLEVELAND

ARPress
45 Dan Road Suite 36
Canton MA 02021

Hotline: 1(800) 220-7660
Fax: 1(855) 752-6001

Ordering Information:
Quantity Sales. Special discounts are available on quantity purchases by corporations, associations, and others. For details, contact the publisher at the address above.

Printed in the United States of America.

ISBN-13   Paperback   979-8-89389-804-0
               eBook   979-8-89389-805-7

Library of Congress Control Number: 2024923299

"Cleveland presents a powerful piece of writing that portrays the author's keen awareness of our sociocultural mores and political environment. Wrought with a light seasoning of biblical conscience, this work offers hope and deep insight into the perplexities of our times."

—Mary O. Burnette,
Educational Consultant

"Like a fine dessert… this story leaves a mellifluous aftertaste."

—Author of *Kalilah*,
Sabrina L. Wright

In the Zone of Changes provokes thought about America's ongoing challenges."

—Yvonne Edwards,
Principal at Forshay Learning Center School

"Granny is a blessing to the William family."

—Reverend Robert Perry

In the Zone of Changes is a relevant and moving story about the problems of youth in our times. This story should be the center of discussion in every home and appropriate classroom, everywhere!"

—Author of *Black Blues and Shiny Songs*,
Tommy S. Young

Kudos from students:

"Fresh language and unexpected twists make this literary novella worth the read."

—Terry E.

"Love, fear, anger, anxiety, and compassion are the emotional changes Brenda William experiences when America takes a new turn in history."

—Helen J.

"The story held my interest and moves quickly. I read it in one day."

—Shirley S.

"Everyone's future is, in reality, an urn full of unknown treasures from which all may draw unguessed prizes."

—Lord Dunsany

For my electronic and spiritual friends,
for your eyes, ears, emotions, beliefs,
encouragements and your *amour* of being in the zone of changes.

Viva! Love

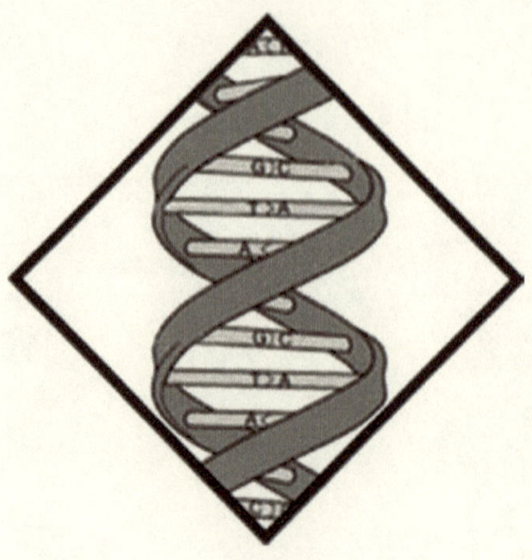

When humans are born, they enter their zone of change with a wail for life. They do not know the order of the universe; they do not know the paths or patterns of their own psyche, fears, challenges, rejoices, failures, and funerals to be created by others, by them, or finalized by God. They do not know the end results of living in a world that changes as quickly as the birth of the next child entering his zone of time to survive and be recognized as a relative to his mother and father's people or his brother or sister or another human being for any number of different types of relationships.

Open is better than closed.
Close turns warmer than distance.
Loving grows easier than spite.
Grudges create more hostility than forgiveness.
Convenience shows more tolerance than being alone.
Being platonic can cultivate rather than destroy.

In a changing world or society, relationships coexist until differences bring about dislikes, disagreements, or disappointments in standards, morals, beliefs, politics or sexual and racial preferences.

CHAPTER 1

B renda William, a young teenager who looked forward to graduating in the near future, sat in her seat listening to Ms. Rutherford's instructions for the class's culminating activity for analyzing *The Metamorphosis* by Franz Kafka. Joseph Charles Madison continued to interrupt the discussion by asking questions. Everyone called him JC.

The classroom reflected solid evidence of each student's progress. Student work exhibited in the room included projects and homework from renowned authors: Shakespeare, Hemingway, Fitzgerald, Baldwin, Walker and Nobel Prize winner Toni Morrison. Novels, reference books, magazines, and newspapers were neatly arranged for student use. On the east side of the tetrad room, four computer stations flanked the wall. Students had created a bulletin board titled *The Metamorphosis* that stood out on the west side of the room.

Ms. Rutherford took roll by sight and started class with the standards and objectives before explaining the activities to accomplish their goals. Giving reference to the school's mission statement when appropriate during class was a routine reminder to the students of their purpose for being in school.

Brenda knew that whenever a culminating activity was assigned, JC asked questions. He did not believe in missing anything relevant to his receiving a good grade. Making notations for her research, Brenda listened and observed her classmates.

Patrick de la Tora shook his head. He tapped rhythmically on his desk with his pencil while shaking his right leg. He seemed annoyed with JC's question.

"I wish he would shut up," Oscar Reynolds said under his breath. "Oh my goodness, not again," Patricia Chow laughed to herself.

Fair with brown eyes and brown hair, Beverly Goldberg sported a sassy asymmetrical haircut. Being from a family that believed in togetherness, integrity, and academics, she took copious notes. Whenever the academic students celebrated an event or planned to do community activities, the students gathered at Beverly's.

Ms. Rutherford, an organized and well-planned certified English teacher, paused and stated, "Write your questions down, JC, and ask them when I'm finished with the instructions."

Brenda had known JC since grade school; she had had a crush on him since the eleventh grade. He was eighteen, in his senior year of high school; and he had turned out to be an academic achiever, an athlete, and was respected by his peers, family, and community.

Known for its high standards and its diverse population, John Nicholas High School consisted of students from affluent to poor. Well equipped for the learning process, the school's staff and its students took education serious. However, a few students took education as a journey's joyride without realizing that not getting an education might have harsh implications on their lives.

The school was named after Major John Nicholas who served in the U.S. Army Air Force during World War II. According to historical testimonies, he was captured during the Holocaust and served time at the Dora Concentration Camp in Germany with other Jewish prisoners. Most students answered JNHS when asked, "What school do you attend?" The school's mascot, a jaguar and the school's red and black colors symbolized courage, determination, and strength.

Ms. Rutherford brought her instructions to an end. "If you have additional questions, now is the time to ask them."

Nicole Jamison asked a question. Then JC referred to his list and asked three more questions for clarification. The bell rang. Ms. Rutherford recapitulated her answer to JC's last question in a few seconds.

Then she gave her final directive. "Class dismissed."

Brenda maneuvered herself through other students quickly. She wanted to catch JC before he left for basketball practice. To her surprise,

he waited for her near the door. He stood in front of her; his fragrance wafted in the air as he smiled.

"I'm excited about our final assignment, and I'm glad you're in my group," he declared.

Me too, she thought. "Your questions were appropriate. Many times, as students, we don't ask questions because we think they're not important."

"Important or not, I'm asking questions," he uttered. They looked at each other and smiled while continuing to walk in the hallway.

JC removed a sports bar and a bottle of water from his backpack. He offered Brenda to break off a piece if she wanted to, but she responded, "No, thanks."

Lockers opened and closed. Some closed with bangs. Students talked in clusters. Sauntering through students, repeating one of the Hall Decorum Policies that had been established by the students, a teacher admonished, "Ladies and gentlemen, 'No Congregating' in the hall, 'No Congregating' in the hall." Instructors stood outside their doors monitoring the students.

"Hey, man," shouted Ronald Pikes, "you better not be late for practice. You know how Coach Morgan is."

"Yeah. Yeah, I know."

"How's your mom?" Brenda inquired.

"Oh, she's better. Her pressure goes up when she eats the wrong foods and when she worries about me and how she'll make ends meet."

"I'm glad she's better."

Brenda had home issues too. Her mother and father loved each other. Her father's grandmother lived with them, and she was eighty-six, had hypertension, and was diagnosed as borderline diabetic. She never said much about her father because his main interest was for her to finish college, and everyone in the family knew that. Many times, Brenda felt overwhelmed by her father's beliefs and behavior. His constant concern caused her to struggle with occasional anxiety.

Benjamin William took pride in his family by being responsible, caring and determined that his only child would be a professional of her choice. The drive for his child to educate herself became a recurring issue once Brenda graduated from junior high. A high school graduate and long jump athlete, he managed to finish two years of college. An unforeseen family matter came into play; he dropped out of school to help his mother by taking a job as a city worker. As a result, he failed to recognize the effect he was having on his child until his wife informed him of Brenda's anxieties and reactions.

JC's father sacrificed his life to save an elderly lady when a bank robbery turned for the worst. Whatever they needed, his mother provided; and whenever she had extra money left after savings and expenses, she bought extra "wants" for him. Most of JC's part time job money went towards his saving for college.

"Gotta go. Text me after seven," JC added, leaving for the gym. JC stopped and turned around to check Brenda out with her light tan skin and black hair in a ponytail pulled up with a banana clip. She possessed a set of captivating brown eyes, strong long arms and shapely legs that supported her Halle Berry-shaped body. He thought: She's smart.

Brenda walked towards the girls' locker room and changed into her practice clothes. Other cheerleaders observed her entrance. The captain of the cheer group smiled and addressed Brenda.

"Girl, I saw you talking to JC. The boy knows he's some kinda fine. I know everybody's seen those triceps and those biceps are a handful to touch. When he walks, he flows in space. Wearing those sunglasses makes him look sooo *GQ*. Are you two an item?" she questioned in a sexy voice, slightly dragging some of the words.

"No, we're not."

"Well, that means he's up for grabs."

"I guess so."

The captain of the squad rolled her eyes back and jiggled herself, making curvy motions with her hands and enunciated, "Details, details, details."

Several cheerleaders laughed. They knew she enjoyed joking around.

"Girls! Come on out of the locker room. It's time to practice," called out Mrs. Cowan, the coach, who believed in starting and ending on time. All the cheerleaders performed warm-up exercises, ran one lap, performed a few more stretches, and then practiced their cheers followed by individual cool down stretches.

An hour and fifteen minutes later, Brenda strolled to the library to check out materials for her assignment. Once in the library, she found useful resources. The notes taken in class made the task easier.

Known for being bizarre and mysterious, Ronald Pikes swaggered over to her. Smart but unsure where he fit in, he hung out with other students from the rival school or the community at large who were less focused than he.

"I know who stole your sweater," he whispered. These words caught Brenda's attention.

"You do? Who?"

He whispered the name in her ear.

"No way! She's my friend." Remembering a student talking about Janis Wilson's stealing her yearbook last year, Brenda thought this may be true. However, Brenda did not believe the rumor at the time her friend had mentioned the incident to her.

"How do you know? Are you sure?"

"I saw it pushed down in her backpack the day it came up missing."

"Why did you wait until now to tell me?"

"I don't know." Ronald's body swayed toward the door. Brenda stared at his back until he disappeared through the double doors. She wanted to run after him; instead she sat in her seat, stunned by the revelation.

Brenda left the library and stopped by the fruit machine and bought an apple. Walking alone, she thought about JC being a handsome young man, but so many girls hang around him. I don't want to be a nincompoop.

Across the campus, she saw two members of her group sprawled out on the lawn. Two squirrels circled around a tree trunk.

"Hey, you guys." Brenda bit into her apple again. "What's up?" they asked.

John Butler wore black and silver glasses that frame his eyes, making him look like a photographed scholar. Josephine Smith had sanguine hair surrounding her lightface with long black lashes curling from her half quarter shaped lids. With long earrings and dark lipstick that gave her lips a solemn smirk, she nodded her head after every comment.

"I got some information from the library," declared Brenda.

"We did too. We downloaded articles from the computer room," stated John.

"Great! When are we getting together?"

"If you have time, we can make a schedule now," John proposed. "Why not?"

"What about JC? You know he and the basketball guys practice after he gets off work on Saturday?"

"Oh, I'll text him later this evening and let him know. I'm sure if we need to make changes, we can," Brenda assured John.

"That'll work," Josephine injected with enthusiasm.

After they finished the schedule, Brenda left for home with thoughts of Janis Wilson who had reportedly stolen her sweater. Janis, like a dandelion weed, stood tall and had a cruel kindness about her being. How could she? How could her mother allow her to keep stolen chattels? Doesn't she know stealing is a sin? She remembered her great-grandmother's thoughts on stealing: If you steal, you will pay.

The cooing of doves in the magnolia tree caught her attention before she entered the living room of her house.

CHAPTER 2

Having discussed her sweater being stolen by someone with her mother and father a few weeks earlier, Brenda decided to drop the issue. Her mom had bought the cashmere sweater at a thrift store, had it cleaned, and surprised Brenda with it at dinner one night after she had made honor roll. With second thoughts, she waited until after class and asked Janis about her sweater.

A short, strict, and midsize woman, Ms. Rutherford held the textbook at waist level while the natural light sketched her head and body into a silhouette across her desk. Before the class ended, she returned essays from two days earlier.

Oh my! We're getting our essays back, thought Brenda.

When JC received his essay, he took it gently, perused it, and said, "Thank you."

"Keep up the good work, JC," Ms. Rutherford advised, moving down the aisle.

Looking over at Ronald, JC gave him a thumbs-up. Thumbs-up in class meant an A. Ronald reciprocated the gesture.

Gee! Ronald got an A. I'm his tutor. If he received an A, I should get one too. I hope I got an A this time, Brenda thought.

A student brought in a summons for JC. He left immediately. "Janis, you need to study more. This grade doesn't reflect your potentials. The tutorial program is available," said Ms. Rutherford.

"I'll do better on the next one," replied Janis. Then she snapped, "Everybody can't make As."

Janis, medium height, and wore braids, enjoyed applying makeup to her chestnut brown eyes and face. Some students called Janis the dandelion weed because of her unpredictable nature.

When Brenda received her essay, she saw a B+ at the top and thought: She laid my paper on my desk. She didn't give it to me in my hand. Oh my goodness! What happened? Why didn't I get an A? What's wrong with my response? Sometimes I think Ms. Rutherford is subjective in her grading. What does she have against me? She nitpicks at my essays. Sweat oozed atop her nose.... Stop. Breathe slowly. Count to seven. You're striving to reach a goal. Be calm but not upset.

Brenda perused the results of her study habits. She felt maybe she could have done better. Questions asserted themselves in her mind: Why is this response wrong? How can I improve my essays? She wrote down the questions in her journal to ask Ms. Rutherford at her next student conference that happened to be this afternoon. Before leaving class, Brenda wrote *WELL DONE* on a sheet of paper and held it up for Ronald to see. Ms. Rutherford issued the rest of the papers and reminded the class that projects were due in a week, and that they would be given class time to complete the assignment.

After class, Brenda caught up with Janis at her locker. In a calm voice, she asked, "Did you steal my sweater?"

"What? Who said I stole your sweater?"

"I asked you a question."

"Whoever said I stole your sweater is a liar."

"You haven't answered my question."

"I have no intentions of answering your stupid question."

"Janis, we're friends. Why get loud? That doesn't help."

Slamming her locker door, Janis scoffed, "Did you steal my sweater?"

"I'm not afraid of you."

Dropping her books, Janis grimaced, "Oh yeah! Then bring it on, girlfriend."

"Thief!"

A few curious students swarmed around them. Others kept walking; a few looked back at the commotion while walking to their classes.

"Liar!" quipped Janis.

"One warning ladies! Let's move on to class. You can solve your differences later. The last bell will be sounding soon. You must be inside the classroom, not out here in the hallway," cried out an adult hall monitor.

Students did not hesitate to enter the classrooms. They knew what being tardy meant—a call home after being tardy three times.

Brenda felt abashed at how she had reacted. It never fazed her that Janis would want to fight over what belonged to her. She wondered if Ronald had lied. Why didn't Janis answer her question? What caused her to get angry? Taking several deep breaths, she proceeded to class with anxiety affecting her body. She sucked a lozenge to relieve dry mouth.

Brenda entered her math class and noticed her name on the board for problem 13. Time used its flight feathers while in class. Interaction between Mr. Garcia and the students was good. Mr. Garcia—distinguished and with a clean appearance—kept his eyes focused on his students' process for solving problems, constantly turning his head like a blue jay as his eyes peered over the rim of his glasses.

"Brenda, it's your turn," Mr. Garcia stated.

She finished her notes for the last problem and walked to the front of the class. She worked out her word problem by reading it to the class, turning to the board, setting up the problem, and solving the problem by using a step-by-step method.

"Now, check your answer."

Brenda explained her calculations to confirm her answer.

Wearing blue jay colors—a blue necktie with a pin-striped white and gray shirt—Mr. Garcia squinted his eyes in a complimentary expression, "Thanks, Ms. William. You used the correct process for solving problem 13."

When she sat down, she realized she had not made the correct effort to solve her problem with Janis. She made a few quick notes about Janis in her math notebook. As soon as the bell rang, she gathered her books and rushed to the counseling office to file a report and request a conference.

After leaving the counseling office, she returned to Ms. Rutherford's room for her student conference.

"Let me print the new rules for using the computers. I will be with you," stated Ms. Rutherford. A few seconds passed, and she continued, "What are your concerns, Brenda?"

"Ms. Rutherford, I put so much effort into writing this essay, and I would like to know why my response to the prompt is wrong? How can I improve my essays?"

"Let's see your essay. Your overall response is excellent. The third paragraph caught my attention. I indicated on your paper the misuse of parallel construction using *and who* and *who*, separating the subject and verb, and a shift in tense."

"I see what the mistakes are. How can I improve my essays?"

"You received a good grade. You're doing well. The analysis is written well. You can improve by paying attention to my corrections, reviewing the rules, and keeping your analysis well organized."

"If my analysis is written well, why would you lower my grade an entire point?"

"Brenda, I didn't lower your grade. You earned what is considered a good grade minus serious grammatical errors."

"I don't recall your stating in class that a student's grade would be determined after consideration of miss using parallel construction of *and who* and *who* when it was not taught in class. On February 10, I took notes on parallel construction, and I found examples of correlative and coordinating conjunctions, comparison and contrast, but not for and *who* and *which* clauses."

"In the next class, I'll do a mini-lesson on these rules for the class. Thanks for bringing this to my attention. Did you read the rule in your text?"

"Yes, the rule is on page 33-D."

"Brenda, I admire your effort, but it's your responsibility to read the chapters, to pay attention to the lessons and to ask any questions when you're not clear about grammatical usage with clauses."

The two made eye contact before Brenda said, "Thanks, Ms. Rutherford. You've answered my questions. I don't deserve this grade." Brenda left while Ms. Rutherford watched.

Clearing the door, Brenda thought: Those errors shouldn't play a part in my grade if my analysis addressed the prompt correctly. I guess the essay didn't meet her greatest expectations. Maybe? Before turning in my essay, I should have read it over again. Semantics: 'The analysis is written well.' Well means good, better, best. An internal battle stirred in her being as she battled with trying not to be upset.

Afterward, she hurried to cheerleader practice. Feeling unsure about seeing Janis, she went to practice anyway. Ms. Cowan accepted her late apology at the door. Completing her warm-up, Brenda joined the rest of the team in their cheers.

A few of the squad members inquired, "What's up with you and Janis?"

Brenda did not reveal any additional information, knowing she did not want to make matters worse. Practice went well.

As Brenda drank from a bottle of water and walked home, she pondered: Problems. Why do people have to deal with problems? She reflected on her personal issues with stress at school; on her father's concerns about his health; her great-grandmother's challenge of surviving each day while struggling with old age and taking twelve different pills a day to treat high blood pressure, cholesterol, borderline diabetes, and arthritis; and on her father's relentless push for her to go to college. I feel engulfed in a wave. Most of us struggle with issues, and the resolutions seem unpredictable and come with much pain. Inside her mind, a word cloud floated (overwhelmed).

A musical jingle played and broke her thoughts. She searched for her cell phone in a side pocket of her backpack and viewed a text from JC.

Are you okay?
Yes, I'm fine. Cheerleader practice went well. Janis was a no-show, she texted back.

A mixture of scents roamed the airwaves of her home. Those scents triggered her appetite. Clara William, known as a good cook and homemaker, cooked wholesome meals. Rushing over to Granny, who was overweight, with hair in disarray from being in bed, dressed in her leisure suit, and sitting stoically in her chair at the table, Brenda kissed her on the cheek.

Granny mumbled, "Love you, honey."

"Love you more, Granny."

"You're right on time, honey. We don't have to wait. Wash your hands and come to the table," enjoined her mom in a caring tone.

"Okay," replied Brenda. Before washing her hands and face, she texted JC the group's schedule.

After blessing the food, Brenda's father asked her, "How was your day?"

She wanted to tell everything that entered her mind, but she did not. Enjoying dinner with her parents she felt was better than getting herself upset again and causing them to worry about her even more. Her mother had told her to forget the sweater when they talked about it several weeks earlier. She had promised that maybe in the future, she might get a new one for graduation.

Besides she and her family enjoyed listening to her father's events of the day. He worked for the Department of Water and Power. Reading meters for the city, he enjoyed telling funny or dramatic stories taking place in the neighborhood in which he worked: a fireman delivering a baby, someone's missing dog returned, old man Pierce wanting him to wait a few minutes while he picked a few more lemons for him, or seeing the migration of monarchs flying across the sky in May, like a magic rug with an invisible genie.

"It went well. I made a B+ on my essay. I'm happy my grade point average will remain the same."

"That's my girl. I know you, and I know there's room for improvement. College is the ultimate goal here," stated her father.

"Yes, I know. I'm looking forward to the day."

"You're not the only one," affirmed Granny. "We've been sacrificing and saving a long time. That scholarhship will help too."

Family members passed around baked chicken with olive oil, onions, and tomato-basil-based sauce on a platter. Brown rice followed with some steamed string beans. Brenda's mom used to cook soul food saturated in butter and highly seasoned with lots of baked breads, but she became concerned about her family's health after the doctor recommended she change their diet because her husband had been diagnosed with high cholesterol; he sported too much fat around his waist. Granny felt secure in medicating her conditions rather than managing her conditions. As a result, her extended life caused her to use a walker most of the time to get around on her own.

Dinner concluded with yogurt as a snack before bedtime or fresh fruit or a few low-sugar cookies and milk for Granny. Usually Brenda drank milk or ate fruit. Many times, she skipped the cookies. Whenever her mom served homemade or store-bought sugarless desserts, Granny would turn her lips up "at that mess." Key-lime cup cakes? "Yes!"

A long day ended with homework and then Brenda relaxed in her room and engaged herself in silence, allowing herself to let go of what she had no control over and allowing herself to be aware, assured in her world, and to gain composure of self in stillness.

CHAPTER 3

Except for detention, Janis rarely missed eating lunch with her friends. Brenda missed her friendliness, even though her attitude would change occasionally. Students put the bottles and cans in recycled bins after lunch. Brenda gathered unopened water and milk cartons. Other students put wrapped sandwiches into a paper bag. Today was Beverly's day to place the bag on the north side of the campus for a homeless man who appreciated the "grub," as the man called their gift.

A strange buzz familiar to bees floated around the tables, or was it a familiar hum like bees floating around the table? An eerie sensation moved in space, causing the mood of the students to intensify. Sitting students jumped up from their seats and ran. Students talking to each other suddenly moved and ran away in different directions. Brenda's cell played "Beethoven's Fifth." She thought. It might be my mom. Brenda looked at her phone screen. Michelle Evans? How did Michelle get my number? She mused.

"Hello."

"Brenda! Hurry! Come to the front of the school."

"For what?"

"Somebody said JC got shot!"

Brenda's voice choked off, "Oh no!"

Sweat crawled on her skin as if it were icy bath bubbles. Her knees buckled for a second. She slipped into *deja vu* and heard confusing noises as her stomach boiled. Between the confusing noises, she heard herself say, "Get control, breathe." Within the confusing noises, within the pull for air, several deep breaths rose up out of her mouth.

"Are you okay?" asked someone who did not stay but continued to run.

"OK. OK," echoed in her ears after she responded.

"Oh my God," she said faintly. Confusion hung in her head with two knots: one for life to be spared and the other for death not this soon.

In seconds, students swarmed all over the lunch area, running, pushing, and shoving each other, trying to rush to the front of the school. Teachers, personnel, and security tried to manage the students. Police cars surrounded the school quickly. Several helicopters hovered above in triangle formation. A blowing, bubbling sound cut the air. The school's PA system echoed with instructions: "This is an emergency. Please walk to your assigned zone on the football field and line up. Wait for your homeroom teacher. Please, do not run. Walk to the football field. This is an emergency."

Brenda felt herself pushing through the crowd and running when space allowed her to run. She reached a gate that separated the lunch area from the entrance to the quad area. Policemen patrolled the area and the locked gate.

"Please, let me through. I know him."

"Sorry, no one is allowed beyond this gate. Everyone go to the football field. Follow the procedures for an emergency," commanded an officer.

"Please!"

Students screamed comments and exclamations, "Let her through! Let her through! Open this gate! We want to get out of here! That's her friend. That's her boyfriend! Pigs!"

Someone pulled her blouse and called out, "I know a way out."

To her surprise, it was Janis. "What did you say? I can't hear you."

"I know a way out!"

"Where?"

"On the north side of the campus, there's a cut portion in the fence. We can get through."

"Way over there! That's too far!"

"No, it's not. Come on. We can make it." She yanked Brenda's hand. Once they reached the fence, it did not seem far when they broke through, ran three blocks, weaved through cars, pushed by people standing on lawns, and avoided trampling on flowers. Dog owners stood, being curious, with their pets. An expectant mother pushed her way through the crowd. Students overflowed in the street, with cops giving firm directions to stay clear of the scene and go to the football field. Traffic in the area came to a standstill. A young man pushing a shopping cart filled with recycled plastic and glass bottles could not move. Standing on cars, people stretched their bodies, trying to see the action down the street.

Police officers stood their ground behind the yellow taped-off area: CRIME SCENE DO NOT CROSS. Red, blue, and yellow lights scintillated from police cars and a fire truck lights added somber to the atmosphere. The S.W.A.T Team remained parked in its armored vehicle, and the team waited for its command. An airplane in the sky let out a prolonged roar going someplace. Brenda ran straight clear of an officer who tried to grab her. Janis stopped at the tape.

"Come back here, young lady! Get back here, now!" the officer bellowed. Brenda picked up speed and did not stop until her water-filled eyes did not believe what they were seeing. JC stood in front of her in a melancholy state. Tears caressed his face, gray and drained. His mouth formed the words "Go back." Blood covered his shirt. Taking longer strides, she reached him, but she could not touch him. Out of breathe and exhausted, she fell to her knees.

"What happened," she panted.

"Miss, you must get off this lawn and get behind the yellow tape, or I'll be forced to arrest you. This *is* a crime scene," quipped the officer.

Students yelled, "C'mon back. Don't let them arrest you! Janis took a chance and ran to her.

Reaching for his handcuffs, the officer yelled, "Move! Now!"

"I got her officer. She's leaving," remarked Janis grabbing Brenda's arm.

They walked away. In her blurry vision, Brenda saw detectives with FORENSIC on their jackets. Knots tangled in her stomach. Saliva secreted between her jaws. Sweat made her hot. She regurgitated:

lunch/ lunch/lunch, before reaching the tape. A camera flashed. To Brenda, JC remained dear in her heart.

Three members of The Guys gang and JC had been handcuffed, and officers proceeded to put them in squad cars. An officer quoted them their Miranda rights: "You have the right to remain silent. Anything you say can be used against you in a court of law." JC looked through the rear window and saw Brenda and Janis disappearing into the crowd.

The Guys did not hang around the school, but they had been seen passing by occasionally. Often it appeared they were visiting someone in one of the houses across the street from the school. Most of the time, they wore blue or black denim outfits with gray or white tee shirts and black or white sneakers. Iconography could be seen on their knuckles, arms and necks. The Guys' overall appearance looked unkempt and disturbing.

On the front lawn of JNHS, the United States American flag furled in the wind. A siren resounded in the distance.

CHAPTER 4

When the door closed, her parents greeted her. Granny sat on the seat of her walker, listening and observing.

"Honey, where have you been? Your father and I've been worried. Why didn't you answer your phone?" questioned her mother with great concern.

"I didn't hear it ring. Mom, there was so much confusion and noise. No one could hear anything."

"Your father went to the school and found out you were absent from roll call after the emergency. Where were you?"

Brenda debated with herself for a second, and then decided to tell them about the events and JC. Her father could not believe his ears were still attached.

"Am I hearing you right? You got a boyfriend? You never mentioned JC to us," he emphasized with deep curiosity. "We're worried about you, and you're at school running to a crime scene behind some JC."

"I know."

"Are you ashamed to bring him around your family?"

"Ben, please!" injected her mother. "She's home now. I'm sure this young man must be special if our daughter likes him. Besides, the students have been through a lot after the shooting. Calm down."

"Okay, okay, I'm calm. What's his name? What do you know about him? Do you know anything concerning how he got himself in trouble?" Making an aside comment, "I'll be damned! We're not sending you to school to get in trouble and to be with somebody called JC. Who is he?"

"His name is Joseph Charles Madison. I've known him since the fourth grade. He's an A student and expects to go to college next fall, and I don't believe he's in trouble. He's not that kind of person."

"Oh, is he Mrs. Rose Madison's son? We know her, don't we, Clara?" he asked, not being sure whether his daughter was talking about the woman they met at the PTA meetings.

"Honey, why don't you go and wash up and relax some. Then go to the kitchen and get yourself something to eat. Your father and I need to talk."

Granny stayed out of the mother-father's squabbles. The family ate dinner without Brenda.

In the mirror, Brenda's mind recaptured some of the events that had occurred. Janis yanking her arm, running, seeing JC leave in a squad car, and talking with Janis before coming home.

Splashes of cold water on her face, neck and arms made her body cool down. Self pats with a towel felt soothing to her skin. Then a slip of her arms into a fresh tee shirt caused her to feel good about being in her room where she could try and sort through this unusual day.

She sat down by her dresser and looked at her father's photo. My stomach feels better, but I'm worried about JC. I'm tired of you repeating yourself and beating up on me verbally. She took several deep breaths and blew them out, releasing tension in her chest. A desire for being comfortable caused her to move and lie on her bed. I don't have anything to be ashamed of by showing my feelings. Why wouldn't my dad like him? I hope he understands that my intentions aren't meant to hurt him. Other thoughts penetrated her mind: Over time students have committed many infractions; but this time, time has stabbed me in my heart. Brenda listened to Miles Davis's lyrical style playing softly from Granny's room. She too could use some relaxing with one of America's most popular jazz icons. Her life was changing like improvisational jazz.

Since Ronald Pikes's arrival at the school about eight months ago, he had been known for several infractions: smoking in the boys' bathroom, starting a fight, and serving detention for playing practical jokes like posting an unopened prophylactic on a teacher's bulletin board based on a dare. He was smart; however, his behavior suggested an inner need: *attention*.

Brenda's mind ruminated in time about one of Ronald's thought to be the most classic of pranks that occurred in Mr. Curtis's history class. Mr. Curtis had a well-shaven, manly face, brown skin, no wrinkles near a fold, a sharp nose, round amber eyes, and teeth sported veneers in his heart-shaped face. He outlined three topics for discussion.

Mr. Curtis explicated, "Each group will have fifteen minutes to present. The final fifteen minutes will be for questions and answers."

Ronald blurted out, "Look! There's a rat under his desk." Chaos did not hesitate to descend upon the room. Students jumped up immediately.

"Where?" asked a student.

"There! It came out of his backpack," yelled another student pointing toward Sammy Quinn.

Students moved around and away from Sammy who had a bedraggled appearance and seemed not to care what others thought. A falling desk added more excitement to the students' reactions. A few girls started screaming and laughing; the laughter took on a personality and caught others up in its wild-joy-for-fun, giggling, bumping shoulders like a quarter back breaking through a hole and heading towards the end zone for a touch down.

"Where?"

"Under his desk."

"There's the rat!"

"Where?"

"Over there!"

"I don't see it."

"It's over there!"

"Where?"

"Over there!"

"Unda yonder!"

"I don't see it!"

"Look! There it goes!"

"It's over there!"

"Where?"

A student kicked Sammy's backpack. No rat was seen. Water flowed from the backpack. "Oh my goodness! Did he pee too?" yelled out another student.

Sammy stood with expressions of multiple questions on his face. What is this about, who did what, and what should I do? The commotion started a few minutes after he had put his head on his desk and fell asleep.

Showing interest, Mr. Curtis inquired, "Where's the rat?"

"It's by your desk."

Laughter spewed and reveled in its good time. Students continued to move around and encourage more chaos. Several girls screamed again and jumped on the seat of their desks. When the noise reached its highest level, an administrator walked in with security.

"What's going on in here?" questioned the administrator firmly. "A rat came out of Sammy's backpack," asserted a student.

"You must be kidding me. Sammy, did you bring a pet rat to school?"

"No, I didn't."

"This incident is similar to the stink bomb released in the boy's locker room last week. Unacceptable behavior will not be tolerated."

The administrator and the security officer marched the suspected culprits to his office. Students meandered in the room until they finally seated themselves after being told several times "sit down" by Mr. Curtis. For practical purposes, history class for the day was over.

Once Mr. Curtis had everyone seated, he said, "The classroom isn't a place for practical jokes, but an environment conducive for learning. Disrupting your class time takes away from your learning. I don't want this to happen again. Have I made myself clear? I want an apology."

He accepted everyone's apology, and he admitted he too had been baited.

A knock on the door broke into her thoughts. Brenda got up and opened the door. Holding her walker, Granny made her way inside the door. They embraced. "I'm glad you are home. We were worried," expressed Granny with a concerned tone.

"I'm glad to be home, Granny."

Granny held on to Brenda's arm for a moment and examined her countenance for her own pleasure of observing her great-granddaughter. With squinted eyes and a concerned look hidden behind a smile, Granny asked, "How are you feeling?"

"Like a rotten apple."

"Can you cut off enough of the bad part for us to share the better part?"

Brenda's response rose from her tight shoulders—through her neck—to her mouth, "I guess so."

"Good. Anything I need to know?"

"No, not really."

"Are you sure?"

"Yes."

"When you came through the door this evening, you looked pale to me."

"Granny, why is Daddy so angry about JC and I being friends? He's my friend. I'm concerned about his welfare. Aren't we supposed to have compassion for our friends? I feel pushed aside like a side dish."

"What did you expect when your father couldn't find you at school? He loves you and expects for you to behave, do the right things, to study, and go to school so you can have a better life than we've had. That is our expectation. You're still your mother and father's responsibility. We love you, and God knows your father doesn't want you to feel pushed aside. Sometimes men don't know how to say what they should be saying because they think it makes them a softie. You should've called. That's why you have a phone. I think you should've mentioned JC a long time ago. I suspected you were talking to someone special."

"I think he's special."

"Well, that means we have two special people to be concerned about." They shared mutual smiles.

"I'm sorry I didn't call."

"I think you need to tell your parents you're sorry."

The door eased open with Brenda's mother carrying a tray. "I brought you some food, honey. You need to eat something."

"I'm not hungry."

"Have you eaten anything since lunch? It's been a long afternoon and evening."

Since her mom mentioned it, she thought perhaps she did need some food. So much had happened; she did not think about food.

"Thanks, Mom." Her mom placed the tray on her desk and looked at her child for a moment admiring how she had grown, the way she was dealing with life, and most of all, her child had empathy for others.

"You know your father and I would like for you to stay focused during your last year of high school. We've talked about you being a young lady and not being distracted by first love, which can sometimes ruin a young woman's life," expressed her mother with tinges of admiration, uncertainty and hope.

"I'm not sexually active."

"And I hope you remain inactive and graduate from high school. Being sexually active means being responsible for you and possibly for the life of another human being. That could put your education on hold for some time. For most, it becomes a dream that fades in the distant past. You know, the STD rate is high among teenagers. Think about it. Are you ready to take responsibility for being an adult with those kinds of problems?"

Granny reached for her walker, stepped her way towards the door and commented, "According to an article I read, STD is high among senior citizens." She closed the door.

With closed eyes, her mother heard the music of Miles seeping in her soul. She felt renewed after imagining previous doubts. Grabbing her daughter and holding her, she advised, "Whatever life presents us with, we must face reality and be sensible. You can always come to Granny, your father, or me. We love you so much. Now eat something. I hope you like the salad with crackers. Be sure to drink the chamomile tea."

Brenda nibbled at the salad. A fear of throwing up again bothered her. Her mother was right the soothing tea and crackers provided some comfort for her queasy stomach.

In the shower, warm water rolled over her slim body. Lavender scents escaped from the soap bubbles, crisscrossing over her coco-butter brown skin, rolling and bubbling their way down the drain, taking away tension in her shoulders, back and leg muscles, away to another invisible entity. Relaxed in bed, Brenda felt better, but her mind tossed thoughts.

Usually she slept well after a shower, but these thoughts played believe-it-or-not with her: I can't believe what I did. Will the police interview me or not? It can't be true JC is involved with a gang. He can't. He's not … I love … . Sleep caught her off guard in her last thought and held her tight like a tree, ever still in sleep at night. Planted deep in dreams on an endless road where her shadow became larger than she, where she grew larger than her shadow, and where her shadow and she merged into one, she slept without waking from her dream. He awakened her in time for school when a train announced its railway crossing with a short, short, long blowing of its horn.

CHAPTER 5

The day seemed white and then gray. Brenda's emotional state lacked luster. Her eyes reflected brown, her mouth chewed gum for dryness, and her feelings pressed an empty hole in her chest. Walking to school was not the same this morning.

Students' parents received phone calls from the school about the tragedy which assured them the campus was safe and the Crisis Intervention Team would be on campus helping students and staff with their emotional needs.

The 440 girls' relay team passed her. As they passed, almost in unison, they greeted Brenda. Another student with them who was not a track member and styled a hootchie mama look was known for saying whatever she wanted to say. A small black tattooed cross on her bicep insinuated belief, belong, or nothingness, thought Brenda.

"Y'all didn't see Brenda and Janis sprinting ta' the scene yesterday? I was smoking a cigarette near the north side of the fence when they pass'd me as if they wer' gazelles running in the wild. 'Em girls can run. Y'all need ta' recruit 'em ta' the track team 'cause 'em records y'all got would be put ta' shame," stated the unknown student with the track team.

Giggling, the last leg runner of the relay team asked, "Why don't you join the track team?"

"Y'all know I don't like ta' run. I like ta' smoke, eat, and do my homework."

Sadness and laughter mingled in Brenda's inner emotions while she inhaled air for life, and the invisible pollution crawled down into her lungs. A honking horn startled her. Beige chill bumps oozed on her skin. She kept walking forward in her provided space. She reached in her backpack for a bottle of water and took several sips.

Rumors roamed in the hallways among the students as they strolled along in the main hallway of the school. Two students talked.

"I heard JC was inside the house," implied one of the students. "He's too smart to hang with thugs."

Overhearing the students' speculative conversation, Brenda commented, "I think you should wait and get the facts," injected Brenda as she passed them.

The students did not know what to believe. After roll was taken in homeroom, students who knew Ronald and felt they needed counseling were told to go to the library. Brenda arrived and took a seat at a table for six or more. Students continued to enter and find seats. Two students from the track team sat with her.

Janis rushed in and whispered to Brenda, "I overslept."

"Glad you came."

One of the girls on the track team spoke to Brenda, "You slipped though that cop's hands quicker than a noodle falls from a fork."

Students talked at random while waiting for the meeting to start. "Did you hear the guys arrested with JC are bangers?"

"Girl, JC ain't no banger."

"I didn't say he was."

"Who knows? One can never tell."

"The Crisis Intervention Team should give us the information we need to know," remarked Brenda. Standing in the library's entrance, JC looked over students' heads, spotted Brenda and strolled over. They embraced for the first time. She felt their simultaneous pull for deep breaths. In low voices, they talked.

"How did it go? I was worried the police might keep you," Brenda looked at him with much concern.

"I thought so too. They were nicer than I thought they would be. I was allowed to wash up, and they gave me a tee shirt to wear. Then they asked me general questions. To my surprise, they released me to my mother after the drug/alcohol tests turned out negative. I'm sure I'm here because I didn't witness the shooting and for not being a gangbanger. I'm exhausted."

"What were you doing in the house?"

"I wasn't in the house."

"We better stop talking. The meeting is about to start." She put her gum in the wrapper to throw away later.

The principal introduced the Crisis Intervention Team (CIT) and what their purposes were. Three speakers spoke. The first speaker spoke on the facts that had been gathered with sympathy for the loss of Ronald Pikes, whose life had been cut short of its potential in the future.

"Ronald Pikes committed suicide. He was playing Russian roulette with a gang called The Guys from another school," revealed the speaker. The speaker continued with factual information from the police report that could be shared with them.

Everyone gasped. Interjections raced around the room in disbelief: "What! No way! Russian roulette!"

"Dang! His guardian angel must have been taking an afternoon nap," commented the hootchie mama-looking student. One of the counselors reprimanded her.

Counselors circulated the room, offering tissues, water, and comforting pats on the shoulders of students. Doing everything she could, Brenda tried to control the grief that filled her chest. Tears filled her eyes, and JC put his head in his hands and shook his head. He reached over to comfort Brenda. Ronald had become a buddy to him, and now he was gone forever.

Hearing it said by someone else made the reality sink deeper into a cerebration of his experience with the officers and the Chief of Police.

"Tell us what happened, and how you end up inside the house?" demanded Officer Tauber.

"While talking to some of my teammates across the street from the school, I saw one of The Guys run out of the house screaming, 'Somebody help me!' Seeing his face, I knew something was wrong. I told my friends to call 911. That's when I crossed the street. As I approached the yard, the same Guy, in a state of confusion, pointed his finger towards the door. I entered. Oh, my goodness. I saw Ronald on the floor. I rushed over. I thought I could help, and I grabbed him in my arms. Thinking he was alive—"Ronald, man, hang on. Hang on.' Nobody wants to die alone. The Guys were not his friends or his relatives. I held him … still warm … but no heartbeat …. I was thinking he deserved to feel that someone was near when his life ended. I just held him. I held him in disappointment and in love."

A short pause ensued. The officers looked at each other.

"And you expect us to believe your story?" The Chief commented shaking his head.

"I'm telling the truth."

"And I got a liquid vitamin in a bottle for stopping death."

"Please, believe me."

"Son, I will believe you when I get the facts related to this case which includes ballistics and DNA results. Until then, I will release you. If you are as clean as you look, then you will not see me in this office again. Do you get my point?

Nodding his head in affirmation, JC asked, "Why would Ronald take his life?"

Not moved emotionally, Janis inquired with a low verbal expression, "I wonder why."

A second speaker continued, "We're here to listen and to support your emotional needs. It's our hope you understand the impact of this crisis, and whatever is said is held in confidentiality. We're here to help you deal positively with your emotions, so you can return to your normal activities with self-confidence."

Students cried, sniffled, offered comforting words, and hugged each other.

Another speaker expressed his heartfelt sorrow. He made a transition by counting off students in numbers for group activities. Within each group, students volunteered and shared stories about Ronald. Many times, laughter scattered about the room. When they finished their stories, they responded by writing about how they felt now compared to earlier. Volunteers shared their responses. Brenda listened to her peers read.

In the afternoon, the groups participated in other activities. JC shared a huge postcard, and everyone in the room signed the card, drew images, stuck stickers, and felt good about their creation. Students smiled, scripted farewell messages, and laughed at some of the responses and images on the card. Brenda's group made red and black ribbons for everyone in attendance, and they pinned them on each other. Sheryl suggested to Brenda to encourage some of the school clubs and organizations to volunteer and make more ribbons for those attending the services. Students embraced each other after pinning each other's ribbons.

The final speaker concluded by asking for volunteers to help students plan what they would like to do to help the family. A few suggestions offered seemed like fun: a car wash to help buy flowers or to make a donation to the family members to help them out or to get the school choir to sing a song at the service.

Mrs. Snearl, the leader of the school's crisis team, stood elegantly dressed, and warmth slipped from her lips, "Young ladies and gentlemen, the activities you have engaged in were designed to help eliminate some of your emotional stress and to restore your spirit for normal activities." Mrs. Snearl reviewed and provided all the students a handout of community resources and addressed a few final questions asked by the students.

After the debriefing, the students felt better about the tragedy and themselves. Few cried. An inner connective spirit to Ronald's transition existed among the students as they prepared for his home going.

The hallways were not as somber as they had been, and the noise rose to its usual level the next day. Brenda was summoned to the office. Going to the office, she felt like she was treading water in slow motion. She desired to float outside and become a cloud. Other students did the rubberneck at her. *The cops are still here. I know I'm about to face a police officer. Breathe deeply,* Brenda thought. *It's okay. Breathe. I wonder what type of questions they'll ask? I don't want to be a witness and testify about something I don't know. My father will burn.*

Someone said something to her. She did not pay them any attention.

Approaching the office, Brenda saw an officer exit the door.

As Brenda entered the office, Ms. Gabbana smiled, opened her door, and reminded her, "You requested a conference about your stolen cardigan, and your parents were able to make it this afternoon. I called your mother this morning, and she called your father."

Seeing her father made her sweat in the pits of her arms. So much had happened in the last forty-eight hours, she had forgotten about requesting a conference. Before the greetings were finished, Janis and Mrs. Wilson entered the office. Ms. Gabbana made sure everyone was seated and introduced the parents.

"I'll get to the point because I'm sure everyone wants to get home for dinner. Brenda, your cardigan was stolen several weeks ago according our records. You checked lost-and-found several times, inquired with other students, and asked Mr. Curtis because you forgot the sweater in his room. I see you had an altercation with Janis in the hallway a few days ago."

The parents seemed to sit with some tension in their shoulders and with their fingers locked together, not knowing what to expect. Mr. William, showing anxiousness, decided to try and figure out where the counselor was headed. "Ms. Gabbana, with all due respect, I hope you're not trying to say Brenda didn't wear the sweater to school."

"Oh no, Mr. William. I know she wore the sweater. It has been found." Everyone adjusted their bodies in their chairs.

In a definitive tone, "I didn't steal her sweater." Janis smiled scornfully.

"Your mother has something to show you," Ms. Gabbana retorted. To everyone's surprise, Brenda's sweater was pulled out of a grocery bag.

Mrs. Wilson asked, "What do you have to say for yourself, Janis? I found it in the back of your closet. I've told you over and over stealing is wrong. You must stop stealing."

Shamed and feeling discomfort, Janis's eyes became watery. Brenda felt Janis's pain and disgust with herself. Mrs. Wilson gestured to Janis with her head and eyes, "Well?"

Gathering her emotions and some thoughts through her tears, Janis mumbled, "Brenda, I apologize for taking your sweater, and I ask you to forgive me." Silence settled around everyone. Janis started a new statement. "I ask that you forgive me for stealing your sweater."

Accepting her cardigan and at the same time elated to see it, Brenda answered, "I accept your apology, and I hope we can continue to be friends." She smiled in the knowledge that Janis was experiencing much shame for her behavior, and she reached out to hug her. Janis turned away. Brenda respected her reaction.

Ms. Gabbana showed gracious respect to the parents for coming and dismissed Brenda and her family.

"See you in the morning," said Brenda after a deep breath.

Janis never turned around to acknowledge Brenda's statement. The Wilsons remained for a private conference.

CHAPTER 6

When Brenda and her family arrived home, she headed straight to her room. Her father had talked most of the way home about her being focused. She was glad her mother told him "ease off " and let her relax some while riding in the backseat of the car. Thank God for mothers, she thought. Brenda missed cheerleader practice for the first time.

In her room, Brenda felt her phone vibrate. Looking at the screen she read:

I need to talk. Call me.

In seconds, she said, "Hello, JC, are you all right?"

"In so many ways, yes, and in so many ways, no. Officer Tauber questioned me after basketball practice. She said they wanted to ask me a few more questions." Silence hung in the phone for a few seconds.

"And?"

Clearing his throat, "She asked me a bunch of questions: Did I ever visit Ronald's house? Did he have a cell phone? Did I ever see him with a gun? I was nervous. One cop took notes. They asked those questions like an M-16 being fired. You know cops can intimidate you."

"Yes, I know." She reflected on the cop she had seen leaving the counseling office.

"Oh my goodness. I hope I don't get questioned."

"Maybe they won't. I don't know. I became uneasy after I left school. I started thinking. I don't need a juvenile record for something

I knew nothing about. I hope this doesn't come down to my mother seeking advice from an attorney."

"Did you ever go to the house across the street?"

"Yes, I did once. I left as soon as I saw those Guys approaching. I never went inside. I stayed on the lawn talking and waiting with Ronald. I wasn't in the house the day of the shooting."

"I think as long as you tell the truth you'll be fine. You can't lie about anything. Once you tell one lie, you'll be forced to tell another." She remembered this from Granny who stated vehemently, "I can't stand a liar!"

"Did you tell any lies during the interview?"

"No, I didn't."

"Good."

"Brenda, dinner is ready," her mother shouted. "Listen, uh … I gotta go."

"Talk to you tomorrow."

"I think you should talk to Mrs. Snearl tomorrow about your feelings."

"Thanks. I will. I'm glad you called back. I needed to talk."

"Take care."

"Okay."

"*Ciao.*"

The Chief of Police, a broad-shouldered once upon a time army sergeant, instructed his officers as they reviewed tapes of the aftermath surrounding the crime scene. Speaking in a New York accent, he verbalized his thoughts: "What do we have here? Have these kids lost their minds indulging in arson, binge drinking, black gold, bullying, choking games, gang banging, and now Russian roulette?"

Watching the tape of the crime scene, the chief pointed at the screen and commanded, "Stop the tape. See the young girl running across the lawn. Find her. Officer Tauber, you take her. Find out what she knows. Who were Ronald Pikes's friends? Talk to his teachers and counselors. Check to see what those students know about Ronald Pikes and any other relevant information that will give us clues why this kid was playing Russian roulette." He flipped through a folder of papers and continued, "Check out any student wearing all-black denim, white or black tennis, bandannas, and iconography on fingers, neck, and arms. Skull bandannas were found in the pockets of the three Guys we arrested at the crime scene."

"Chief, we checked the address on the school registration card. The place turned out to be an empty boutique shop. This kid might be a long-time kidnapped victim or another kid raising himself.

Another officer conjectured, "He could be homeless or a runaway."

"Officer Schneider, where are the cell phone and computer data information on these Guys?" quipped the chief. "On your desk, sir."

"Great! I will review the data after we finish here. I want you to interview a roach if it looks suspicious to you. Somebody knows something about these miscreants," declared the chief strongly.

The doorbell rang; Brenda thought: Oh, good. Some of our relatives are visiting. They're the only ones who come without calling. When her father opened the door, an officer looked at him.

"Good evening, Mr. William?"

"Yes," he answered with a puzzled look on his face. "I'm Officer Tauber. Is Brenda William home?"

"Umm … yes, she's here. Ahh, come in," he said as he looked from the opened door to see another officer standing by a squad car. He called Brenda.

As Officer Tauber stepped into the doorway, she observed a modest, clean, and organized home. A couch and a love seat graced the living room with family photos atop a console. Three comfortable chairs rested at angles fitting for holding intimate conversations around the couches. Standing tall in the left corner of the room, a mahogany bookcase was filled with reference books. Several African art pictures and masks that had been placed on the walls and other items of interest caught her attention.

"Thank you. I would like to ask her a few questions about Ronald Pikes."

Clara stood at the division of the living room and the dining room.

Brenda entered the room with enthusiasm, "The personal pronoun is here." No one laughed, but Officer Tauber smiled. Seeing the police brought about a perplexed look on her face.

The officer resumed, "Brenda, I'm Officer Tauber. This won't take much time. Mr. and Mrs. William, sorry for the interruption, but we must get information as soon as possible when a crime takes place."

Brenda's mother noticed everyone standing. "Well, let's have a seat."

Brenda's heart chased beats, and her voice trembled similar to a rose petal shaking from a brief breeze. She did not know what to expect. The officer fired a few general statements: state your name, age, address, and phone number. Brenda reached in her shirt pocket for a lozenge. Officer Tauber moved into more specific questions.

"How long have you known Ronald Pikes?"

"I've known him about eight months."

"Have you ever been to his house?"

"No, I haven't."

"Do you know where he lives?"

"No, I don't."

Brenda's mother poured a few glasses of tea and served them. Brenda took a few sips to soothe her throat. Officer Tauber continued to record her answers on an iPad.

"Do you have a cell phone?"

"Yes."

"Have you ever texted any messages to Ronald Pikes?" Looking directly at Brenda as she swallowed a few sips of tea.

Brenda's eyes fixed a stare straight at the officer. Her breath heaved from her stomach as she answered, "Yes, I have."

"Good Lord!" her father exclaimed in a low voice with dissatisfaction. "Did you call once, twice or regularly?"

"I remember calling JC on his cell once to deliver a message to Ronald."

"Do you remember the message?"

"To remind Ronald to be on time for tutoring. I didn't know Ronald had a cell phone."

"He didn't have one. What do you know about The Guys?"

"Nothing. I saw them walking by the school sometimes. None of them said anything to me or my friends."

"Officer Tauber, I think we should stop here. The last few questions are suggesting to me we may need an attorney present," stated her father firmly.

"Mr. and Mrs. William, Brenda has been cooperative, and if our investigation warrants an attorney, we'll be the first to agree." Officer Tauber took a few sips of tea before leaving and expressed, "Good mango tea, Mrs. William. Thanks."

Holding her business cards in hand, Officer Tauber gave one to Brenda's father. "Call me if you need to do so. This information is for our personal records. Thank you for your time. Have a good evening."

As soon as the door closed, Brenda's father turned around and released his frustrations. "I've told you to stay away from trouble. What's happening to you?"

"Dad, please . . ."

"This family has made some huge sacrifices for you. It looks like you're about to throw it all away behind JC, thugs, and your friend, Janis, with her 'issues.' Do you know I was docked three hours for leaving my job to attend the conference with Ms. Gabbana and your mom? A squad car was parked in front of our house. Unbelievable! Do you know what this could do to your reputation, to this family, to your future? What if you need a lawyer?"

"Dad, I . . ."

Infuriated, her father continued, "Don't let your dream slip away from you by one tragic or unfortunate mistake. Nothing is more important than an education. We want you to make good choices in your life. You're only a few years from being recognized as a professional. I missed my chance. I chose responsibility, and I have worked hard to live a life with dignity and to have a respectable family."

Silence managed to catch a moment. "Dad, let me explain."

"There's no explanation! You've done so well until this year. You need an education. Do you understand me?"

With tears flowing, Brenda affirmed, "Yes, I do."

"If this is what they call senior *'itis*, I don't want to see or hear any more of it in this house."

Emotionally affected by her father's rejection, Brenda put her face in her palms as uncertainty circulated in her mind about school, her relationship with JC, and the way her father was reacting. Shame covered her being so much she could not seem to lift herself off the couch. She felt like a large piece of dead bark beside a long road to nowhere. She wept.

"Ben, please, can't you see the child doesn't need you to ...?"

Pointing his finger at his wife, he declared openly, "Clara, I'm tired of you taking up for her."

This moment came to a halt when Brenda's mother did not flitch and demanded her husband put his finger down with her body language. Brenda's father looked around; he snatched his hat off the hat hook.

Slam! Down the steps, he mumbled, "Might need a lawyer," in disgust. Off he went into the night.

"Benjamin knows better than to point his finger in my face up in here," vocalized Clara.

CHAPTER 7

The silver clouds suspended themselves like upside down nets. Brenda figured Janis was too ashamed to face her so early in the morning. Maybe that's why she did not come by as usual. Brenda reflected: How strange nature is when it desires to be unaccountable for its actions, but we humans are held accountable for our actions. Blue jays lifted their wings quick, alert, and without a sound. Sheryl, who lived around the corner, joined her in her walk to school.

Some students ate their breakfast on the way to school. Another student read a book as he walked. A few students sipped on drinks from Starbucks. Others joked around, girls put on lipstick and fixed their hair; boys stood around checking out some of the girls' *derrieres*, legs, and *chee-chees*. Buses pulled to the curb, unloading students who lived some distance away. A few of the students listened to their iPods, talked on cell phones and texted messages.

In the hallway, a student ran by Brenda. "I guess he doesn't see the 'No running' sign on the wall," observed Sheryl.

"He might be in hurry," replied Brenda in a monotonic voice that suggested anyone could not see or may forget the rule if he were preoccupied with thoughts. Mozart's *Sonata for Two Pianos* played softly as students entered Ms. Rutherford's class and took their seats. Ms. Rutherford completed writing class information on the board. When the tardy bell rang, the monitor closed the door. From the chalkboard, she reviewed the standards, the objectives, and the tasks at hand. She allowed them ten minutes to reflect in their journals before class ended.

"Today, class, you'll use this time to work on your projects. Use your time wisely. Some of you've been working with the Crisis Intervention Team, and I think you could use this time to get ahead on your projects," instructed Ms. Rutherford.

Everyone thanked Ms. Rutherford and proceeded to get busy. Josephine, John, JC, and Brenda squared off their desks and started removing notes, books, articles, and flash drives from their backpacks. Ms. Rutherford circulated and answered questions, clarified confusions, and monitored groups and the computer stations.

Completing a follow-up session with the CIT after their English class, Brenda, JC, and other students learned that Ronald Pikes had been homeless. Exactly where he lived or how he had been surviving was under investigation according to an officer who spoke at the meeting. Students shared their final plans with the CIT for assisting in the home going celebration in loving memory of Ronald Pikes at the Toland United Methodist Church. Apparently, extended family had arrived, and funeral arrangements were being made for Tuesday morning.

"You're going to experience the mourning stage after Ronald has been buried. There'll be times when "the moments" will sneak up, and those moments will demand separation because your friend and classmate, Ronald Pikes, is no longer with you. Letting go emotionally will be your time of grief. During the next few months, you'll miss him the most. This time is for you to overcome his death, dissolve your attachment, and let life continue with its light of consciousness for you to learn from Ronald Pikes's unfortunate demise. Please, don't forget, if you need additional support, contact your counselor or use your community resource handout or talk to your parents about your concerns. Additional handouts are available on the table, if you have misplaced the one given to you earlier. I'll be here the rest of the day, if anyone needs to talk to me personally," concluded Mrs. Snearl.

Students returned for the Friday night basketball game. Once everyone cleared security check, the crowd moved to the spirit of the team they supported. This game was dedicated to Ronald Pikes. The

Jaguars played the Bobcats, the school's rival. Wearing their red and black ribbons, the basketball team looked anxious to challenge their rivals, the city's champions. Students, teachers, administrators, parents, and community members made up the audience. The gym was packed to its capacity. A few policemen monitored areas. The choral club sold ribbons for fifty cents for the purchase of a wreath.

An excited crowd participated with much enthusiasm. Each team came out, and the starters were announced. Jump ball in center court became a control for JC. He started dribbling toward the Jaguar's goal for a strategy set up for himself or one of his teammates. After several passes and five seconds left on the clock, one of his teammates popped a long three pointer.

With every ball possession, the audience stood up and cheered, "Yeah!" Others in the audience shouted.

"Bingo!"

"Money, honey!"

"Swish!"

Many attendants clapped their hands, made dancing moves, and spilled popcorn while doing so.

In seconds, the Jaguars placed themselves on defense with the Bobcats. The crowd yelled, "Defense! Defense!" Jaguar fans got quiet when an opposition player executed a slam dunk on a pick and roll. Visitors cheering for their team screamed, "Yea!"

Everyone present showed excitement at halftime. The score? Tied.

Brenda and the rest of the cheerleaders performed a cheer that included Ronald's name. Janis had not been seen for several days and had missed all of the activities for the game, as well as the activities planned for Ronald's funeral on Tuesday morning at 11:00 a.m. In the interim, Brenda had been voted head cheerleader.

At the beginning of the second half, JC and his teammates tightened their defense. Team members rebounded when the ball was shot. They cut down on turnovers. They made every effort to make sure the opposition did not rebound as much as they had in the first quarter. Conversions at the free throw line increased for JC and his teammates. More shots fell through the hoop during the third quarter.

The Jaguar's mascot danced and clapped his hands, encouraging the audience to sing: "So glad to be a Jaguar. So glad to be a Jaguar."

Drummers in the school's band hit the drums with a quick triple beat: Boom! Boom! Boom! The rival team's head cheerleader yelled commands for their students and visitors to respond:

"Give me a B."
"Give me an O."
"Give me a B."
"Give me a C."
"Give me an A."
"Give me a T."
"Give me an S."
"What does that spell?"

"Bobcats! Bobcats! Bobcats!" screamed the crowd of the rival team in a syncopated rhythm.

One of the team members on the opposite team fouled JC as he scurried to the basket with a pull-up bank on the board for two points. Simultaneously, the referee shifted himself in position to see the players while blowing his whistle. Tied game again (80 to 80 flashed on the scoreboard). Both teams executed well. The opposition team observers made noises so loud only a few in the audience heard the whistle. Nervous, palms sweating, heart pounding, JC shot the ball. He converted. A hush fell on the crowd.

Coach Morgan stood six feet, and he looked distinguished in his suit and tie at the game. He wore walking shorts most of the time at school. He relished the compliments he received for his shapely legs. Signaling for a time out to draw up a play to stop the opposition from scoring on an inbound ball, he shouted, "Time out!"

After the short discussion, he admonished his team, "Stay focused! And execute!"

Time started ticking.

Defense with a block shot allowed JC's teammate to catch the ball and pass it to him. With fifteen seconds left, JC hand signaled the final play with an opponent full-pressing him across the centerline. A clear-out took place; he dribbled to the left and then to the right, came back center, looked at the clock, focused, and pulled up, releasing the ball into a three pointer.

"Nothing but net!" screamed his mother from the audience. If the audience had not known any better, they would have thought they had seen Kobe Bryant make a final nonchalant shot.

Everyone stood up and cheered in unison, "Yeah!"

When the buzzer finalized the game, JC's team members jumped on him, showing their togetherness in an eventful conclusion. Cheers of joy thundered through the gymnasium; students pranced down the bleachers and high-fived up streets. The school's band played, "Whoop! There it is. Whoop! There it is." During all of the excitement, JC and the rest of the Jaguar team shook hands with the Bobcats.

Once he was free, a crowd of girls surrounded him similar to a hive.

Dialogue cut cross the space in which they occupied. "JC, what a shot!"

"Fantastic! Can you believe it? We won!"

"Meet us at Beverly's. She's having a party."

Those comments sounded good to his ears, but he was not focused on their attention.

"Thanks. Thank you. I need to get dressed," he said smiling. "What a game!" He pumped his fist in the air.

One of the girls in the crowd shouted, "You got that right!" Laughter followed.

He looked around for Brenda. He rushed over to the cheerleader bench. "Sheryl, where is she?"

"Brenda left with her father after you were fouled."

He could not believe she left. Questions scrolled his mind: Why did she leave? What could have happened? He wondered if she had texted him, but when he got to the locker room, he checked his Recent Calls—Empty.

CHAPTER 8

Brenda and her father drove to the hospital. Having received a text: *Your father will pick you up after the game* and a cell phone call from her mother at halftime, Brenda decided to meet her father at the gymnasium's entrance.

Entering room 625, Brenda asked, "Mom, what happened? Granny was all right when I left for the game."

"I know. I went to the grocery store to get some fresh fruits and vegetables for the weekend. While I was gone, she got sick; and she used her medical alert system to call paramedics. It's her heart."

"Oh, I'm all right. Come here," said Granny, extending her arms. Granny gave Brenda the usual hug without lots of strength. An empty hole suddenly opened atop her stomach as if something was missing. Losing Granny would put a void in her life. Losing Granny would mean losing her best friend. Pressure mounted in her chest. Her face became blushed. Seeing her granny with several intravenous tubes and an oxygen tank near her bed made her think the worst. When Brenda released Granny, her hands started shaking; she lost her balance for a few seconds.

"Sit down, Brenda. Get some water, Ben. Continue to breathe deeply," commanded her mother. He poured water from a pitcher into a glass on the nightstand by Granny's bedside.

Granny did not believe in hospital gowns. Brenda's mother had brought Granny's personal gown with a pink-laced top and with a Nehru-style collar that buttoned down the front to the waist. Her hair, pulled back, showcased her face looking pale but pleasant, still smiling with a beam in her eyes.

"Was today a better day," Granny asked Brenda.

"Yes, indeed. My group's project is coming along fine. We'll meet tomorrow morning at the library to finish. The basketball game was at a tie when I left. Based on the loud noises we heard when Dad and I left, we won. Students standing outside screaming, 'We won! We won.' I'm so glad for JC and the team. Oh! I am thinking about joining the track team."

"That's wonderful," stated her mother.

Immediately Brenda realized she had been talking to Granny like they were in Granny's room at home. Her father did not hesitate to express himself. "What about your studies?

"My GPA is 3.8." Brenda commenced to feel warm.

"I think you need to raise it a little more. That's the problem adding extracurricular activities to an already full academic schedule." He emphasized extracurricular activities with a touch of anger as he looked at Brenda to get her on an eye-to-eye level with him.

"Ben, she's doing fine. Brenda, we are proud of you. Ben, the doctor has told me exercise releases tension, stress, and gives her a sense of well-being."

With emphasis on every word, he replied, "She does not need to exercise more. She needs to exercise her brain into a sense of well-being."

"Mom, do you mind if I get something else to drink?"

"Yes, a good idea."

As soon as Brenda left, her mother addressed her husband, "Ben, calm down. If you keep this up, you might have a heart attack. Just let Brenda grow up and be the young lady and student that she is."

"Clara, I don't . . ."

"She's our daughter. We need to continue to support her and help her by having less stress at home. Think about what she deals with at school, her classes and grades, her friends, other students—and you."

Granny paid them no attention and was glad Brenda had removed herself from the room. Brenda's father threw up his hands and became sullen and quiet.

The family rode home in silence while the radio played jazz. Brenda enjoyed the music. Each turn of the wheels and the gentle sway of the car helped her relax. She leaned her head back while humming a few notes. Her open arms allowed her to escape into the rhythmic sounds that soothed her into a comfortable sleep. The trip home was peaceful and pleasant. When they entered the house, Brenda checked her cell phone. A text popped up: *Why did you leave the game? Call me after the group meeting tomorrow.*

After Brenda's Saturday morning run, a shower, and breakfast, she headed to the library to meet her group members. They were about fifteen minutes into their collaboration when JC strolled in with a huge smile on his face. John got up. Brenda and Sheryl smiled as they watched the fellows do the hand jive.

"Wow! Man, the team was outa' sight last night," expressed John. A hand shake followed.

"We kicked butt." They bumped fists.

John responded, "Man, the team was in sync with the defense." He made a few quick foot moves as if he were on a basketball court. "What are you doing here? I thought you had to work."

"I did, but the manager was kind enough to let me off for four hours with pay. It was his way of helping out, so I could come and study. He said he didn't know Ronald, but he thought I would appreciate having the time to study. Not only that, he attended the game last night."

"I think that was nice of him," expressed Brenda. JC leaned over and rubbed her shoulder. Flashing a quick smile, he acknowledged Josephine. "I think so too. Mighty nice," he replied, looking deep into Brenda's light brown eyes one-on-one and heart to heart. "Congratulations!" she whispered. "Did you get my message?"

"Uh hum. I'm glad everything's okay."

"Aight, you guys. Let's think themes," prompted John.

The group collaborated and agreed on quotes to support themes found in the text: isolation, rejection of love/lack of love, and the dictates of society. Remaining engaged, they spent their time discussing details while organizing and clarifying the final presentation of the Jigsaw assignment. They focused on the characters, settings, plot structure, and figures of speech. As a group, they reviewed the checklist of their expectations based on a four-point rubric. They all agreed. Josephine would set-up an online collaboration for them to exchange ideas in the next few days. After the meeting, they walked outside, sat on the lawn, and ate lunch.

Brenda's mom fixed enough for her to share with the group. All the grapes, tangerines, veggie cheese slices, and the wheat crackers disappeared. Having a popcorn conversation, they talked and laughed about incidents and classwork. The discussion ranged from low unemployment and underemployment to dealing with Korea and to the city not dealing with local infrastructure. Enjoying and listening to some of their comments caused Brenda to relax and learn more about national and global issues.

Brenda reminded Josephine, "Don't forget to e-mail Ms. Rutherford our meeting log. I think I should be going. I told my mom we would be finished by two o'clock."

"I'll walk with you," smiled JC.

They passed by the grocery store and saw another student they knew leaving the cleaners. A teacher hurried towards her car after leaving the neighborhood bakery. Old man Pierce walked his dog, and the two of them chatted about funeral ideas, homework, her granny being in the hospital, assignments, and the possibility of his asking her father about a date to the movies. At this point in their conversation, Brenda did not think it was the right time.

Arriving at home and entering the living room, Brenda was glad her father had left to see a friend.

"Was that JC?" her mother asked. "Yes, I told him I was proud of him."

"Seems to be a nice young man. Mrs. Richardson attended the game last night, and she told me he is an excellent basketball player and academic student."

"Yes, he is."

"When is he coming for a visit?"

"Not soon. I don't think Dad is ready to accept him. I've thought about inviting him to dinner one Sunday afternoon."

"Why not? I've been talking to your father. You know, he is beefy."

"I'd feel awful if JC came and Dad refused to talk to him or refused to have dinner with us by leaving before he arrives or asking JC so many questions he'd wish he hadn't accepted my invitation—how embarrassing."

"Do you think he would?"

"I guess not, but he might open an umbrella in the house."

"You're your granny's great-grand child," they laughed. "Keep the dinner invite in mind."

Holding fragrant flowers in a vase, JC sauntered into room 625 with a bouquet. Mrs. Edwards looked surprised when she opened her eyes, and her eyebrows flowed upward as her lips parted a radiant smile.

"Mrs. Edwards, these are for you," JC said in a pleasant tone.

Giving him a grateful look, "Oh, thank you sooo much. It's been a long time since a young man brought me flowers. Have a seat, please. Am I right in saying you're Joseph, also known as JC?"

"Yes, you're right. How are you feeling?" He placed the bouquet among the other plants and flowers.

"Better than burnt toast. Brenda talks about you now. She thinks the world of you. She's delicate and unspoiled like the flowers you brought me. If you love them and take good care of them, they stay beautiful for a long time. If not, they wither all too soon. You understand what I mean."

"Yes, ma'am I do."

Examining his face, she continued, "I am glad you came. You have a serious look. Anything on your mind, young man?"

Silence did a quick glide into the room for a few seconds.

As if struggling for the right words, JC started, "Mrs. Edwards, I like Brenda and would like to take her to a movie. I don't want to upset her father by saying something wrong. Do you think he might be open to me asking him?"

"That's a good question, young man. If you like Brenda, you should ask her father your question. Men stand up for what they want, for what they have, and for what they must do."

"I see, Mrs. Edwards."

"Those roses are lovely, and the fragrance makes the room smell like spring. Thank you. Thank you."

"I'm glad you like them. It took awhile to find the perfect bouquet."

"JC, you've had the courage to come here, didn't you?" She gave him a long upward look over her reading glasses, suggesting he could ask Brenda's father for his permission.

"Yes, ma'am. I understand." Looking at his watch, he continued, "I would like to stay longer, but the next bus is coming in a few minutes. I need to get home early this evening. I appreciate your advice. I'll come back to see you. Bye."

Granny waved good-bye, focused on the beautiful flowers, smiled, and closed her eyes.

CHAPTER 9

Every member of the William family attended church on Sunday unless one of them was ill or Brenda's father needed extra rest after working overtime. For lunch, her mom served soup and half sandwiches. Later in the evening, the family planned to go to dinner. In the afternoon, Brenda reviewed sections of her report and printed a final copy from her flash disk. After reading over the report several times, she texted Sheryl.

JC wants to take me to a movie, but my father will probably say no.

If your father says no, then slip off and go.

Are you out of your mind? My father would have a basketball. No.

If I slipped out, my father would get upset if he found out later. My mother—and don't mention—Granny would be disappointed in me.

Have you thought about asking your father?

I think it's the young man's place to ask."

Yap! You're right. My mom is calling me. See u tomorrow. Oh, don't forget to respond to Beverly's blog. She has a new poem for us to read.

Okay.

After a nap, Brenda thought about Sheryl's idea.

At a restaurant, her father and mother's conversation switched from fast-food contributing to obesity and serving as a substitute for hunger, to a disagreement on cultural practices. They talked about the President of the United States marching to his own drummer because he's the leader, not because he's wrong, not because he's educated and strong, but because he's an honest, fair and compassionate man.

The ambience of the dining room allowed people to encounter some change from the regular routine of dining at home. Quiet, soft piped music played. Sipping on ginger ale, her father switched the conversation. "When was the last time you saw JC?"

"Yesterday."

"Mrs. Richardson spoke very highly of him."

"Oh, she did?" Brenda did not let on she already knew. Her father had great respect for Mrs. Richardson and her husband.

Her father recommenced, "They raised three children, and all of them finished college. One of her sons became a doctor; the other became an attorney. Her daughter taught school in New York City for several years, made it as principal, and she's currently Superintendent of Schools."

She thought may be her father might be open to letting JC take her to a movie.

"You know, what her children accomplished was phenomenal. Accomplishing one's goal means sacrificing and not losing your focus." Changing the subject, "I can tell you have some interest in this JC."

"Dad, I'd like to in—"

"Your mother and I know what's best. You just turned seventeen; you're still too young to start dating. I think you should wait until after graduation."

Brenda's mother interrupted, "Ben, did you enjoy your salmon?"

"Yes, I did, Clara. If I hadn't known any better, I would've thought you cooked the meal."

They laughed. Brenda's father gave her mother an endearing look and embraced her. A pleased smiled blushed on her mother's face. The waitress surveyed the area to see if anyone needed refills. Brenda placed her hands face down on her lap and heeded her thought: Not now.

Granny was pleased when they entered her hospital room. A few church members sat in chairs near the foot of her bed. They chatted while watching a television show with no sound. Light bounced off the flowers, and the scents wafted around, under and into their noses.

"Wow! Granny, you've enough plants, cards, and flowers to start a florist shop," commented Brenda.

"That means I'm loved and thought about by my family and friends. Put yours over there next to the bouquet of red roses."

Greetings among the guests and the family held spiritual harmony. The guests used this opportunity for them to leave. Granny's face revealed being pleased that they had come and she said jokingly, "Don't do anything I wouldn't think about doing." Everyone chuckled as she finished expressing herself, "If I don't see you soon, I'll see you later." She waved with a flicker of her fingers.

Brenda and her family spent quality time with Granny who recalled a memorable event in her life.

"I was working at an army base in Colorado. I applied as an experienced waitress. But, they gave me a job cleaning tables. You can't imagine how upset that made me. Once I started working, I noticed I was the only black working in the cafeteria.

When President Theodore Roosevelt came to visit the base officials, I was selected as one of the women to serve him. Only two women were cleared to work the room where he was going to eat. I was dumbfounded that I had been chosen.

Well, they took us to the dining area and locked us in for an hour before he got there. President Theodore Roosevelt and his entourage came in and sat around the table. A guard stood outside the door. Whatever they wanted they asked us servers.

President Roosevelt asked me, 'May I have some more warm bread?' 'Yes, sir.'

I knocked on the door and told the guard who stood on the opposite side of the door. The guard ordered the bread, and in a few minutes it came, and the guard knocked on the door. I took the bread, served it to Mr. Roosevelt. He said, 'Thank you,' in a kindly manner.

Granny continued after a pause, "The President of the United States said thank you to me. After dinner, we had to stay in the room an hour before being released to go home."

She looked at the flowers and plants. Then she looked at her family, winked her eye and commented, "Them other people got hired over me, but I got to serve the President."

Granny was scheduled to return home on Tuesday.

The next day after lunch, Brenda, Sheryl and other students gathered food for the homeless man. Brenda ran over and put the bag outside the gate. When she left, she looked back and saw Officer Tauber putting the homeless man in the squad car. She wondered: What has he done? He never bothers anyone.

As soon as her English class ended, Brenda made a point to walk out the door behind JC.

"I saw the police pick up the homeless man this afternoon," she averred.

"Well, you know the cops have a job to do."

"That's right. I sure hope they don't call on me anymore."

"Don't worry." Flashing his smile, he winked, rubbed her shoulder, and sprinted off to basketball practice.

Dressed in jeans with a dingy blue shirt and a shabby jacket, Mr. Pikes sat in a chair behind a table with a bottle of water in a Spartan room with a mini-camera used for covert viewing. Since he was not a suspect, his Miranda rights were waived. The Chief-of-Police and Officer Tauber questioned him. He needed to talk, and he rambled some.

"I told him not to be with 'em boys call The Guys. He didn't listen. Them boys wuz up to no good. He had a mind of his own. I don't know. Why wouldn't he listen to me? He seemed . . ." said Mr. Pikes.

"Why should he listen to you, Mr. Pikes?" the Chief interrupted. He took a long stare upon his hands and responded with passion,

"I'm his father. I kept telling him to stay in school. Make somethin' out of yourself. He had good friends at that school. Those kids helped him. They got him involved. What do you call it? Oh, tutoring program and his grades started going up.

He thought a lot of JC. Both on the basketball team. And 'em cheerleaders, they good kids 'cause they kept us alive 'cause many times we didn't have no food. Them kids didn't know me. They knowed the child they wuz helping, but they didn't know they wuz helping him. He liked being with me more 'n being with his mother. I don't know where his mother is. I don't know. I got a brother who's arranging things."

"Mr. Pikes, what happened?" inquired Officer Tauber.

He shook his head and took a few seconds before answering. "We left Chicago . . . came to California with the hopes of me finding a construction job, but that didn't pan out. Economy shut down. I got stuck. We been homeless for the last eight months . . . been sleeping in my van. I sleep in the front seat; my son . . . slept in the back . . . more room in the back for a growing young man. This world can chew up a man, spit him out; and he becomes a dead man wandering in society."

"Where were you when the shooting occurred?" asked the Chief.

"I wuz at Hall and Hall Construction site working a day job I picked up earlier that morning. Seem like every time I thought I wuz g'tting' ahead, somethin' come along and knock me down again. He needed more than I had to give. I saw hope in him. And now? And now, I see…. My son wuz around future scholars. To none wuz he able to relate in order to save him from this tragedy." He broke down emotionally. Officer Tuaber handed him a small packet of tissues.

A solemn quietness fell over the church when the organist played a hymn, and Pastor Lewis Toland proceeded with words of grace as the family members entered the church. Two scriptures, one from Psalm 28 and the other from 2 Timothy 4:6-8, were read. A prayer followed the scriptures. Then several teachers, students, and family members reflected on some of their positive experiences with Ronald. JC read a farewell poem:

> *"… This young man's life much too thin.*
> *Cut short too soon, once in full bloom*
> *with the zip on his backpack,*
> *with a high-five after a game,*
> *with 'See ya later, man,'*
> *with a whisper of 'switch' on the court, and*
> *with a thumbs-up in class.*
> *This young man's life much too thin*
> *Once in full bloom, cut short much too soon."*

A copy of the poem was given to Mr. Pikes, the homeless man, whom JC and Brenda discovered from Ms. Gabbana was Ronald's father. Brenda introduced herself and made sure Mr. Pikes and Ronald's extended family wore red and black ribbons on their left shoulders before they entered the church.

A school wreath stood among the many flowers and plants that flanked the brown closed casket. Scripted letters of *So Glad To Be A Jaguar* stood out on the wreath's red ribbon. One of the church members read the obituary and those in attendance read silently. The school choir sang "What a Friend," and they marched to their seats clapping their hands and chanting, "So glad to be a Jaguar."

Ushers circulated the aisles giving out fans and programs. Ceiling fans cooled the air. Inside the church existed a sweet and bitter smell. Odors flourished around red roses and sweat; perfumes and scents of dead spray lingered and stuck to bitter grief. Stale air bit into the smell of chrysanthemums and carnations with a bitter sorrow.

Pastor Toland delivered his message and ended his liturgy with advice to those in attendance: "Now is the time for us to turn to the Lord. Your solace can be found with God. 'Blessed are those who mourn, for they will be comforted' Matthew 3:4. He will see about you. He will give you peace of mind. He will 'wipe away every tear from your eyes' according to Revelation 7:17.

"Don't question Ronald Pikes's death. That's not your job. The real question is what do you do now with your loss and your pain? Now is the time to talk to someone you trust, stay engaged with family and friends, and be involved in constructive activities, relax, read consoling literature and self-help books, and seek professional help. Set goals. Get and stay spiritually centered. Negate negativity. Aim for being optimistic and successful in life. Self-inflicted death shouldn't be an option."

Pastor Toland's voice took on a musical lilt as he continued, "Young people, try not to make the facts of life a problem. Take steps to solve problems that concern you emotionally. Eat properly, exercise often, rest and take breaks and never hate or harass anyone. Now is the time to read your Bible, to feed your spirit, not to become a fanatic, but to acquire and practice decent values. Live in the now, for now is all you have. Now is time to uplift your fellow man by sharing with the hungry and lifting up the downtrodden."

A few in attendance confirmed, "Amen, preach Pastor, you telling the truth."

"Three of the biggest problems in our society are that we're not staying calm, not listening to each other and not being fair with each other. Ronald Pikes tried to change. The streets can capture you like Red River, mesmerizing, tempting you to trust in its mistrust, pulling you under while being lured by your own desires, sucking out your breath; and you surrender your life to a dead end. Now is the time to remember Romans 6:4, because it clearly says the death of one-reality serves as a resurgence to a new dawn, splendid for you to envision, for you to walk, and for you to live in the path of righteous! Amen, Amen, AAAmen," ended Pastor Toland.

Listening to Pastor Toland, Brenda thought of death as a fact of life similar to living in the past and worrying about the future. She had been working on solutions to help her cope, and as a result, she was gaining control over her anxieties. She acknowledged agonizing over the past and trying hard to live in the now. Realizing if she continued to deal with her problem in a step-by-step way 'in the now,' then her problem would not defeat her. Brenda made connections to Pastor Toland's message on Ronald's death and his message on how to help her and others. Tears flowed. Her tears moved tension from her muscles, yet gave her a feeling of inner strength she had not known existed. She thought about the mistakes she made while trying to get her cardigan back and in dealing with her father. She realized this sermon gave her much insight into her future life.

Another member of the church read the acknowledgement, followed by directions for the internment and the repast at the church's hall. At the end of the benediction, a recessional occurred with the congregation singing "Soon and Very Soon."

In an instant—quicker than a snap of the fingers—a restless child started wailing a "Let me outta here, can't you do something, take me outta here" wail that echoed: hard and long; then the sound slammed against the walls of the church and upon the mosaic pane with Christ carrying the cross. The child's mother took him outside.

As Mr. Pikes walked behind the casket in the recessional, a void-red and white-existed inside his chest marked by pain. The pain of his son's absence hit his chest, and before he could get control of his loss, grief consumed him. Tears rested on the rim of his eyes, making vision blurry, causing images to fuse, and making life at the moment seem unbearable. Within his pain, death came out of nowhere … white; and his life remained.

Blood flowed through his heartfelt loss, sounding in a suck for air, trading off a cough while tears broke loose from his eyes, settled into the pours of his face, slid away from his cheeks to spots on his white shirt. He wiped at grief with both hands while his trembling fingers moved as if thin fibers floated over his eyes, or a few hairs brushed against his forehead, or a spider's web swayed across his face. A deep-throated, inarticulate groan escaped over the family's spray, a bleeding heart atop the rolling casket. Once outside in the light of day, he waved his right hand in the air about something not being right, around something he could not touch, and about some things not being right, not his loss .… . Please, change things.

At the entombment, Janis and Brenda stood on opposite sides of the casket. Both finally looked at each other simultaneously. The space between them reflected distance and their differences. One motivated for college; the other motivated by pleasures and good times, creating a raucous, jesting, and experimenting with life's interdictions. Both turned away and departed in separate directions. Brenda reflected: Last year, we were the best of best.

For breakfast, Brenda took her time and ate a bowl of hot oats topped with fruit. Her glass of milk was not too cold. Her mother set it out earlier. She knew Brenda liked her milk best at room temperature.

"I think the students did a good job of planning for Ronald's funeral, and I think the Crisis Intervention Team knows how to bring out the best in students who are grieving. At the repast, when the co-captain presented the winning ball signed by each of the team members and Ronald's jersey to Mr. Pikes, he smiled," remarked her mother.

"I'm glad you came. Ronald was special in his own way. We miss him. Our lessons come in changes, Mom."

"Yeah, I know. Granny was discharged at 10:00 a.m. I would've felt awful had I not attended. Your father was kind enough to pick her up. Right or wrong, your father isn't a man of small convictions."

She and Brenda shared the moment by looking deep into each other's eyes. Brenda recognized her mother had used one of her vocabulary words (convictions) in a sentence correctly.

"Thumbs-up for using the word, Mom. Ms. Rutherford would be proud of you." Both laughed.

"Well, what do you expect when your mother and father study with you? Granny brought back more stuff than she took. You know, those red roses are from JC?"

"What?"

"She told me he rode the bus uptown to see her."

"Did you tell Dad?"

"No, you can tell him if you like."

Her mom kissed her on the forehead and picked up Granny's breakfast to take it to her room. "Enjoy your day, Honey."

CHAPTER 10

Time for giving their presentations in English arrived. Being second from last, the group moved to the front of the room and set up.

"Our group will be discussing themes of *The Metamorphosis*. Kafka presents a preposterous plot. One of the main themes is man's struggle to find meaning in his life and in his personal relationships," stated Josephine.

"The five themes we'll discuss are rejection, love, lack of love, dictates of society, and isolation," expressed John.

He passed out copies of the handout he had designed with the themes listed. JC set up his laptop for the Power Point presentation. Josephine filmed the presentation with a stationary camera belonging to the English department. Accompanying symbols (an apple, a bug, a question mark, and a door) showed on each frame as Brenda and JC alternated turns using quotes from the text to support the selected themes. Students referenced in their texts as pages were announced and explanations were given for each symbol as it related to the themes.

The final theme flashed on the screen: isolation. Brenda read, "'The door was slammed shut with the cane, and then at last everything was quiet' (p. 20)." The door represents Gregor's being alone and being separated from his family."

"What about the cane?" Ms. Rutherford asked.

Brenda resumed, "Umm...Kafka uses the cane as a symbol of Gregor not having unconditional love from his family. The cane reinforces the themes of separation, isolation; and his death in his room alone. I think the cane shows Gregor not receiving proper care, not being a real family member, and not being treated as an equal, but being treated as a lower class animal or bug."

"Good. Proceed."

Using literary and real-life examples, Brenda and her group members proposed questions for their classmates to reflect on in their journals.

"In conclusion, isolation is self-selected or society elected, and as human beings, we'll be challenged with some of the same or similar obstacles Gregor faced. How many of you have felt self-estrangement and thought—Why am I learning calculus? It will not be important in my life. How many of you wished Jay Gatsby in *The Great Gatsby* had stayed isolated? Did anyone desire for Gregor to leave his room? Didn't Gregor imagine himself a bug after he lost his job?" concluded Brenda.

"Do you remember Hester Prynne in *The Scarlet Letter*, who experienced isolation, wearing an *A* for adultery and being alone?" asked Josephine who continued with more questions. "How many changes have our bodies gone through since our birth? From Gregor's perspective as a bug, insect, or vermin, we see a glimpse of how man must deal with mental and physical changes and how man's relatives may treat him when he becomes ill or has ailments or becomes an octogenarian. Who controls your body and its evolutionary process of change? Do our bodies really belong to us? Think again."

"Have your parents experienced the IRS adding penalty charges to their taxes, and have you sensed their feelings of helplessness because of the IRS's power?" John inquired.

"Have you seen where computers, iPods, religion, or sexuality can isolate people? What about viruses like Swine flu, tuberculosis, hepatitis, pneumonia or infectious mononucleosis?" JC questioned.

Brenda asked the final question, "Have you ever felt isolated because of your ethnicity? In our research, we discovered that pain is the metamorphosis of self through virtues: Because courage, temperance, truthfulness, friendliness, and justice are some of the highest attributes man can possess. This concludes our report."

Ms. Rutherford smiled, "Engaging and thought provoking. Good job! Next group, please." She passed the scored rubric with 4 circled to Brenda. The class applauded.

A classmate who was openly gay expressed his feelings, "Kudos."

Still feeling good about her group's presentation, Brenda had a bounce in her step as she approached the gym for cheerleader practice. Mrs. Cowan was absent. A substitute replaced her for the day. On the other side of the field, the substitute teacher talked to another teacher. Janis had returned to school after her suspension. Janis did not say anything to Brenda all day, and Brenda did not force herself to talk to her. To Brenda, it seemed that avoidance was best. In the locker room, Janis approached Brenda and leaned against her.

"What are you doing?" Brenda asked with much interest and skepticism.

Fear asserted itself inside Brenda's being. Her heart took a seat on her tongue, and nervous sweating roamed in places unannounced to her while trembling.

"Is your memory bad, Brenda?"

"I told the truth."

"Who told you I took your sweater?" She jeered. "Janis, I have my sweater, and you apologized."

"Well, this is going to be your truth." Janis pushed Brenda on her right shoulder, and Brenda almost lost her balance wobbling backward. The noise caught the attention of the other cheerleaders. Fear undressed itself and turned into an agent for survival.

"Settle down," warned Brenda.

Before she could say anything else, Janis swung her fist at Brenda's head. Moving quick enough to miss the hit, Brenda's instinct made her like a jaguar. She jumped back. Janis charged forward with an open palm and slapped Brenda across the face. A stinging sensation penetrated her cheek, and in seconds, fear removed itself from the scene. Brenda lunged into Janis, grabbing her right arm, bending it behind Janis's back and throwing her left arm around Janis's neck in a chokehold. Kicking Janis in the back of her knees lightly, Brenda brought her down to her knees. The maneuver occurred so fast Janis did not know what had happened.

"Help! Go get security!" Brenda yelled. "And hurry!" Janis relented, "Okay, okay."

Several cheerleaders started running and screaming, "Help! Fight! Help!" Soon as they turned around heading to the door, the substitute, another teacher, and security arrived in the locker room and separated the girls.

"I didn't start the fight. She did! She choked me!" Janis cried out.

Using a few minutes to catch her breath, Brenda remained still. She splashed her face and her head with some water from a fountain near the door as she walked away.

Both girls were escorted along with several of the cheerleaders to the counseling office. Separated upon arrival, Ms. Gabbana asked questions and listened to each of the girls retell what they had witnessed. The other cheerleaders were dismissed. Janis received a transfer and was instructed to change her behavior if she expected to finish high school. Ms. Gabbana called her mother to pick her up.

"Brenda, don't let this fight bother you. You've experienced what many students have encountered. I'm glad the two of you didn't injure each other seriously. I'm so glad you didn't choke her. You knew what you were doing in that aspect," ended Ms. Gabbana.

Excitement over what had happened prevailed among the students who stayed on the field reminiscing.

"Girl, did you see that? Brenda brought the dandelion weed down!" exclaimed a student in amazement.

"I didn't know the girl had it in her. What a she-cat!" inserted someone else, making a loud cat growl.

"And when she put the chokehold on Janis, I was like—This can't be real," expounded a cheerleader standing on her toes with her arms up in the air and fingers spread wide.

On her way home, Brenda's emotions dropped similar to a fallen cake. She did not think she could deal with the pressure of her father. Now she had a fight to add to his list of dissatisfactions. Inside, she felt proud of defending herself and that she did not let her shield down to be beaten and humiliated for something she did not start nor lie about. Ronald rested. Now she struggled with hopes of life's fairness. She thought about what Granny told her once: Some things you have to take to your grave.

Walking in the doorway greeting her parents and Granny, Brenda put her backpack down. Each responded with brief expressions. Her father gave her a curious look when he peeped over the newspaper. Her mom circled the table setting glasses in place. Granny sat in her chair working a Sudoku puzzle. Brenda washed her hands and returned to help her mother at the table. Her mother moved about in her gentle way, humming a tune. Once she stopped, silence had its moments among the family members. When the table was set, the family assembled to the table and said in unison after the father's blessing of the meal, "Amen."

"Did you have a good day, Dad?"

"My day? What about *your* day? Ms. Gabbana called. We had a three-way phone conference."

Brenda's mouth became spit-less. She reached for her glass of water and swallowed several sips. Silence in the room seemed *ad infinitum*. She managed to recall the events with some humor. A few laughs passed around the table; however, her father did not laugh at the details shared.

"I think Ms. Gabbana handled the situation with objectivity," interposed her mother.

"Clara, please, no interruptions. You've had an altercation with Janis, you ran past a police officer onto a crime scene behind some boy, you've been interviewed by a police officer, and now, you've had a fight with Janis. When are you going to stop doing things that aren't relevant to graduating? You shouldn't be spending your time fooling around. Is there anyone else bullying you at school?"

"I can't say when. The events have happened. I haven't been able to prevent them, nor have I been able to avoid them, Dad."

"I never thought I'd experience this with you."

Recapturing her train of thought, "No, no one is bullying me. I don't see Janis as a bully. She's my friend who has issues to resolve, and her frustrations are being taken out on me because of what she believes is unfair."

Brenda's father had not thought of the altercation like Brenda. He dismissed her point of view. "I'll be glad when graduation is over. You're beginning to make me nervous," he declared. In an aside, he repeated, "Issues," in an insinuating tone, and asked, "What is next?"

"Dad, I'll graduate. I promise. Mom, this stew is good. Pass the bowl, please."

"Mark Twain said 'All you need in this life is ignorance and confidence and then success is sure,'" quoted Granny, continuing "Put the bowl over here when you finish, Brenda."

"I'm surprised at you fighting. However, in life, we never know what challenges we'll face. We must face them responsibly and stay the course until victory is yours," commented her mother.

"I agree. What I'd like to know is where did you learn to do a chokehold?" inquired her father with a lighted face.

"I saw the maneuver on television and said if I ever get in a fight, I'd fight and use it as one of my strategies until help came. It worked. Actually, I amazed myself."

"When will it end?" mumbled her father. He ladled a few more scoops of stew, looked at his wife and commented, "You can tell when a woman cooks with love."

Even though Brenda was forced to defend herself, her first fight would be one she would remember for the rest of her life.

"Surprised? Not me. That took courage. It takes courage for friendship, courage for love, and courage for survival," stated Granny. "I remember my first fight—"

CHAPTER 11

By not excusing herself from the table this evening, Brenda faced and answered all of her father's questions. She did not rely on her mother's help or seek her to smooth things over. She noticed she had eaten most of her dinner and desired more. A physiological change had taken place with her while she dealt with her anxieties. Many of the signs had not occurred recently.

Her father's dominant presence faded as she observed his face. Her beloved father sat before her in his space among the living and the inanimate, living bravely, living with self, during the change of silence, during the change of time. She realized that he desired for her what he dreamt for himself, and he had not accomplished his dream because he had not sacrificed and did not possess the tenacity to do so. He had taken his 'fact of life' and made it his problem.

Later in the bathroom, Brenda poured Epson salt into a tub of warm water. She slid her long slender body down into the water. Jazz played, and with every effort, she released tension from her neck, shoulders, and extended her legs to the length of the tub. With eyes closed her body relaxed with the temperature of the water cooling. She thought how Granny knew what she was talking about when she told her a story once about how she had a fight, and her mother told her 'Child, all you need is a salt soak, and those muscles will loosen.'

Reclining in the tub, she mulled over what arrives after pain? I guess more pain. Without dead leaves, many times, yellow never bursts; yet, blue skies downcast in gray to purple to black, smoking color clouds turn white and bright, refinishing into new visions above serrated mountain tops. After the pain arrives, I know relief.

Several days later, JC walked Brenda home again. Stopping at a self-serve yogurt shop, Brenda selected red velvet cake and vanilla topped with fruit, and JC selected dark chocolate topped with almonds and fruit. They found a table off to the side where fewer people sat.

"I've decided to ask your father myself on Saturday," revealed JC.

"Oh, when did you make that decision?"

"After my visit with Mrs. Edwards."

"I was wondering when you'd tell me."

"C'mon, I didn't have to."

"I don't think it's such a good idea."

"Brenda? We've talked about this before."

"And I've told you how my father reacts."

"I can't let your father cause me to panic and not do what I think is right for me to do." His eyes examined her face, and with his masculine instinct, he touched her hand. He raised his other hand and brushed her hair aside while his heart filled with compassion.

"Your father can't be that bad. We beat the Bobcats, didn't we?"

"My dad isn't the Bobcats."

"You're right, but he's an opposition."

After swallowing a taste of her yogurt, she resumed, "He's alone in the afternoon. My mother and Granny are gone. I usually go with them. Granny looks forward to her outings with us on Saturday. She gets a kick out of operating her scooter."

Brenda's hesitant but pleasant smile reflected in JC's eyes. They finished their yogurt. Pacing their way through two people who wanted their seats, they left. When JC left her at the edge of her yard, she wondered: What if her father said yes? What if her father said no? The final thought made her quiver.

Brenda's early three-mile run on Saturday morning brought her solace. The time supplied her with extra energy and allowed her to release anxiety and to float through the gift of space freely. The sight of running squirrels, a truck uttering a stentorian, and a few cars roamed the neighborhood. Butterflies hopped from flower to flower. Birds chirped and broke the silence.

As Brenda paced herself into a comfortable run, her personal affirmations surfaced: I can be calm but not upset, free but not seized, prodigy but not mediocre. I will use solutions to resolve problems, I will deal with now; and I will strive for peace.

Once the lawn was cut, his truck washed, and the family had left for their outing, Brenda's father relished being in his recliner. Clara had taken his grandmother for a ride to the mall. Peace in his house meant reading the newspaper, watching a baseball game, taking a nap in the afternoon, and being alone with his wife sometimes. He had gone to get a snack from the refrigerator when the doorbell rang.

Opening the door, he saw a tall, Ivy League-dressed young man. "We're not buying anything if you are selling something," stated Mr. William.

"I'm not selling anything, Mr. William. My name is Joseph Charles Madison. The students at JNHS call me JC."

"Well, come in."

"It's a pleasure to meet you," said JC. He extended his hand, only to have his hand rejected with a quick turn of Mr. William's body.

Brenda's father extended his hand toward the couch, "Have a seat, JC. Brenda isn't here. She went with her mother and my grandmother for a ride to the mall. My grandmother enjoys going for a ride to church or even to the mall. She's proud of her new electric scooter. So what's on your mind, JC?"

Silence did a flip. Within his flip, Brenda appeared in the room.

Although Brenda had taken a chance on staying behind, she felt better than being a brown ladybug outside, scampering around under a blade of grass, avoiding a turning blade from catching her.

"I thought you went with your mother," her father stated with a surprised tone.

"No, I needed to finish some homework. I'm going to take the bus and meet them at Macy's. While completing her homework, Brenda decided JC and dad should be alone based on Granny's suggestion: "Let men be the men."

"Good."

"For you." JC handed her a red long stem rose. He thought she was gone, too. He had planned to leave the rose for her. Mr. William watched.

"Thanks. It smells lovely; it's beautiful. I'll put it in some water." Silence and awkwardness booked a few more seconds after she left. "Well, what's all of this about?" questioned her father sitting down in his recliner.

"Mr. William, I'd like to take Brenda on a date with your permission, of course."

"Where?"

"To a movie, Sunday afternoon."

"And if you don't get my permission? Then what?"

"Then we'll wait until after graduation."

Returning to the room, Brenda placed the rose in a vase on an antique French console table. Leaving, Brenda said, "Bye."

"Oh, I see. *We* have it all figured out."

"No, sir, we don't. I'd feel better if I had your permission."

Leaning forward from his chair, "Look son, I'm a loving father and a hardworking man; and I support my family so they don't have to want for anything. Brenda and you are graduating in a few months. She can't be distracted by puppy attraction."

"Mr. William, we have been friends for several years, but recently, we felt an attraction to each other. She's a good person. I promise I'll be respectful, take her on the date, and return her home safely."

"Brenda is too young to be trusted with someone who plans to assume responsibility for a few hours. I'm responsible for her 7 days a week, 24/7 and 365 days every year. She's in this house before eight o'clock on school nights. If she's out any night, I pick her up to make sure she's safe."

Silence played a few notes with itself (time marked in black seconds).

Benjamin William's mind whipped butter. He stared at JC. Moisture appeared. Sweat flowed from his temple. In locked eyes with JC, he stressed, "Let's talk serious talk."

JC thought in broken English. He ain't the Bobcats. He planted his feet deep into the carpet and maintained his eye contact with Mr. William.

Mr. William remained stern and stipulated, "I don't want you to think you can run in here and pick up my daughter a few times to use her then disappear. Both of you need an education, not a "hit and miss" chance in life. Do you understand me?"

"Yes, I do. That's why I asked to take her to a matinee. I thought that would be better since we both will be going to school on Monday, and we have projects to finish."

Keeping a sharp eye on JC, he specified, "I want to make sure we're on the same page, son. Nothing can happen to Brenda. She's a decent young girl; I don't want to hear, see or feel anything bad about my daughter that an irresponsible young man has done to her. Son, do you smoke, drink, or do drugs?"

"No, no, I'm clean. I'm not focused on bad habits." Tiny beads of sweat crawled at the nap of his neck. Underneath the sweat, his neck muscles felt tight. Sitting became uncomfortable, but he kept his spine straight.

"What about this trouble you're in?"

"Mr. William, I have to wait 'til the investigation is over. Until then, I'd like to try and be the student and young man that I am."

"Um huh." Being straightforward, he continued, "Brenda was not a mistake on the lake. Her mother and I were married two years before she came. I hope you know what to do and what not to do."

"Oh, I understand, Mr. William. I respect you and your concerns. You remind me of my father. He had one mantra: "Stay in school, and don't mess up anybody's daughter."

"I respected your father. His loss to our department was tragic. As a matter of fact, I attended his funeral. He trained me and became my supervisor, a good man."

"You worked with my dad?"

"Sure did." His eyes connected with JC's. "Then you know my father kept his word?"

"Oh, yeah, he kept his word." Reflecting he repeated, "A good man."

"My father always told me, 'Your word is your bond. Any man who doesn't keep his word isn't a man.' Mr. William, I'd be betraying my father's faith in me if I lied to you. I promise, I'll bring your daughter home just like she was when she left for as long as we're not married." They stared at each other for what seemed like forever. Then Mr.

William spoke, "There's something special about you. All right son, let's see how the first date goes."

With a sigh of relief, JC pulled in a long breath, stood straight up, and articulated, "Thank you, Mr. William." As Mr. William rose from his recliner, he extended his hand towards JC. They shook hands.

Brenda, her mother and Granny returned from their Saturday outing. As they entered the living room, Granny smiled, "It's good to see you, JC. Come here and give Granny a hug. He put his arms around her, and she whispered, "Did you ask your question?"

He replied quietly, "Yes, ma'am, Mrs. Edwards."

"And?"

"What are you two whispering about?" asked Mrs. William with a teasing smile.

Granny still smiling said, "Thanking him for the roses."

"Mr. William granted me permission to take Brenda to a movie tomorrow afternoon," announced JC.

In a mild tone Brenda uttered, "*Touche*!" Brenda felt revived in her spirit. One of Granny's words resonated in her head—courage. A feeling of being a spring flower poking through dead leaves emanated from her body. She and her mother shared pleasing glances, but her dad stood at attention like a general with a focused look upon them and a blush of a smile creased his lips.

"Here, we bought you something while you were looking at shoes for the prom, stated Granny.

Mr. William shifted his body and had an introspective thought: Round 2, the prom.

Taking the bag, Brenda opened it and pulled out a new cashmere cardigan.

"Thank you, Granny and Mom." She hugged both of them and embraced her father.

"It will keep those shoulders warm while you're in the movies," inferred Granny.

"And those hands in check," commented her father.

Feeling better now, JC flashed his smile, "May I have some water, please."

There existed a genuine rule of law in everyone's mirth, and the path taken would be aligned in the zone of changes.

CHAPTER 12

Reading inspirational verses, praying, spending quiet time and family time together, blessing their food, and being thankful for their blessings—these occurrences meant nothing to some people, but they meant everything to the William family. Anxious yet happy, confident but a bit unsure, Brenda held excitement in her heart for her first date. After lunch with her family, she changed her clothes.

JC texted her: *Will pick you up at two.*

While waiting, Brenda used her wait time to write a rough draft of her essay for *The Great Gatsby*. The outline and the first draft were due Monday. She placed a period after the last sentence a few minutes before two o'clock.

"Good afternoon, Mr. and Mrs. William," JC said entering the living room.

Withhereyesfocusedon JCandhercardiganlaidoverherarm, Brenda entered the room before her parents could finish their greetings.

Her father said, "You look lovely, Brenda. You and JC have a nice time."

"Thanks, Dad."

Reaching a bag to Brenda's mother, "These are for the family. My mother bought roasted almonds from the Farmers Market and thought you might like a bag," said JC.

"How thoughtful. Thank you for bringing them to us. I'm sure we'll enjoy them, especially Ben who never gets enough of them."

"Are you ready?" JC asked Brenda. "Yes."

"Mr. William, I will bring her back safely."

"I believe that, son or you wouldn't be standing there." He smiled

"Would you like to go, sir?"

"No, son. It's your first date. I don't need to chaperone."

As Brenda and JC sauntered down the driveway, her father watched JC open the car door for his daughter.

"Nice car. I didn't know you had one," said Brenda.

"I don't. It belongs to my mother. Do you know when we graduate from college, we'll be able to buy a flying vehicle?"

"Get all-out."

"It's true. I hope to own a Terrafugia sport aircraft in the future."

Brenda's father raised thumbs-up to his wife when JC closed the door. The sun stretched its arms out into a yellow-red sunset. It hovered above the trees a long time before dark.

Clara looked at her husband with ease in her eyes. With a glint in his eyes, her husband gave her a pat on the shoulder and whispered, "I think they'll be just fine.

While in homeroom, Brenda received a summons from Ms. Gabbana. She listened to the announcements. Then she moseyed her way to the office.

"Young lady, do you have a pass?" asked a hall monitor.

Brenda flashed a pass. Wondering what this could be about, she felt confident about being able to handle the situation. With a bounce in her step and her ponytail swaying in silky movements, Brenda announced her arrival and took a seat.

"Come in, Brenda. I'd like to be the first to tell you. I received my list of students who have been accepted to various colleges and universities. You've been accepted at Harvard," stated Ms. Gabbana with delight.

Brenda's mind thought: Believe?

Inspiration filled her body. To herself she rejoiced: Yes! I believe. "Oh my goodness. Oh my goodness," she exclaimed in passionate feelings with her eyes full of tears.

Before leaving the office, she called her mother. No answer. The recorder play: *Please leave a message after the tone.* "Hi, mom, I've been accepted at Harvard. Bye."

Leaving the office, she ran towards JC's class. This must have been her lucky day. The door was open. Feeling a vibration in his pants pocket, JC checked his cell underneath his desktop: *I'm standing in the doorway. I've been accepted at Harvard.* Smiling, he mouthed, "Way to go."

His teacher inquired, "What are you doing, JC? Everyone knows the rule for cell phones. You get one warning." Brenda took off running to her class.

Another hall monitor admonished, "Walk to class. Stop running." Many other seniors found out about where they had been accepted.

The day carried excitement in the voices of seniors, in the voices of teachers, in the voices of administrators, and in the voices of proud parents and relatives.

At the end of the day in the living room, Brenda and her father had a chat. "Brenda, I'm proud of you. I've been overbearing. Your mother and I are able to see you're capable of being whatever you want to be in life, provided you remain focused. So many young people today are losing their opportunities. They seem to be concerned with the moment and not with staying the course for a good education. We've all been worried these last few months. I know I've been guilty of contributing to your anxieties. Your mother and I've been talking, and I am trying not to be so overwhelming. I want to understand your point of view sometimes. Many times I don't recognize what I'm doing. I want to be right most of the time, and when I desire to be right, I get frustrated. I lose control and may think irrationally," said her father with much love. With wisdom far beyond her years, Brenda replied, "Learning to recognize the triggers that cause you to lose control is the best thing you can do for yourself in this life,"

"You'll make a good doctor," praised her father. "Really?"

Granny entered the room pushing her walker. "Did I hear we might have a doctor in the house?"

"Dinner is ready," announced her mother happily.

"Call me doctor!" Brenda commanded enthusiastically with a clap of her hands, and then extending her hands with clenched fists above her head.

A buzz sound occurred. Brenda opened her cell and read a text from JC.

I received two letters of acceptance at Harvard and Yale. Viva! Love.

Several months later. In the same kitchen and around the same table, Brenda finished her breakfast.

"Enjoy your day. Here, your father marked this article for you to read," said her mother leaving the kitchen.

"Oh thanks." Brenda took the paper and read the article marked for her attention.

Student Initiation Goes Awry

By Randy Slater

The Upbound Post

Upbound, CA—A 17-year-old student committed suicide playing Russian roulette Wednesday afternoon at 2417 Lead Street with gang members of The Guys.

Ronald Pikes, who attended JNHS, was recognized at his funeral as a student who seemed to be trying to stay on the right path. His peers and teachers revealed he played basketball, embraced being coached by his peers to improve his study habits, but he remained a mysterious and secretive student to many of them. He and his father arrived in Upbound in September of last year.

Frank Botello, Mark De Soto and George Sanders, members of The Guys gang, were arrested and officially booked for aiding in the suicide of Ronald Pikes. The suicide occurred when Ronald Pikes agreed to be initiated into the gang to become a hook. The Guys members' bail was set at $1 million. All three members had previous convictions: weapons offenses, prior arrest on mail fraud and fencing.

Joseph Charles Madison, other students, and community members provided relevant information during the investigation. None of the students interviewed were charged, nor was anyone placed under bail. Ronald Pikes's classmates will miss him, number **12** on the team of the Jaguar.

When she finished reading the article, she laid the paper down. Silence did not deny her a few seconds of relief. She texted JC the news before leaving for school. Grabbing her backpack, Brenda rushed out the front door. She exhaled.

Envision an American family at home having dinner like the William family living in their designated time zone, in their triangle of life, in their changes within the framework of their unconditional love for each other, and one is forced to deal with how elusive time can be in one's zone of challenges. With no desire to wait or to terminate, time moves in its space; and it never asks for permission to stop. In a changing world or society, relationships coexist with time. Time, an illusory medium, takes on an internal predisposition in man's life—sometimes favorably, sometimes unfavorable in transitions or situations. Sometimes positive, sometimes negative challenges occur in transitions; and sometimes the challenges yield decisions, sometimes truthful and sometimes falsely. In a changing world or society, the formal colors of black and white make time, and change occurs for the worst or best of times.

Perched, healed, delighted, love ever ingrained, the doves outside seemed to coo a psalm with transitions. Have a listen.

Engaging Readers

Discussion

1. Find evidence in the story of the following themes: love, compassion, family, courage, determination and strength.

2. Discuss the relevance of time and change as it relates to the story. Be specific with examples.

3. Relate the story to your life by making connections to other works (novels, movies, operas, Bible, philosophers, current events).

4. Brenda encounters a series of challenges and obstacles. Discuss one encounter or obstacle that impressed you the most. Why? Give three reasons.

5. What is your favorite line, quote, character, or passage? Why?

6. You're a casting director. Cast the main characters of the novel for your movie of the week, and tell why the actors are appropriated for each role. What songs are appropriate for your movie?

7. Compare and contrast two characters of your choice.

8. Select a scene that expresses a philosophical, psychological, physiological, social, economic or political point of view. Read it. Then discuss it with a peer, teacher, classmate, friend or parent.

9. Explain how the title relates to the book.

10. Were you satisfied with the ending? Why or why not?

Do You Have Any Questions?

Write 4 or more questions that you may have about the story.

What if…?

Why…?

Why not…?

How come…?

Would you explain…?

Suggested Activities For Planning

These are merely suggested activities that may be used with *In the Zone of Changes* if planning a lesson around Howard Gardner's multiple intelligences.The activities suggested allow for differentiated instruction. Use appropriate content standards and activities for grade levels 9-12.

Linguistic: See it. Read it. Say it. Learn it. Use it (**Speaking Application; Organization and Delivery).**

Spatial/Visual: Students connect to printed texts, charts, and graphs (**Literary Analysis, LA).**

Engage in Note Taking and Highlighting Text in Personal Books. Design Power Point Presentations and Word Walls. Use Overhead Projector, Handouts, Graphic Oganizers (GO), Make Posters or Brochures. Write Articles, Letters, Editorials, and Résumés.

Interpersonal: Students ask questions for clarification, express beliefs and different perspectives (**LA).**

Engage in Book Talks. Interpret Jigsaw. Analyze and Use Reciprocal Teaching in Literature Circles and Small Group Discussions. Reflect in Double Entry Journals. Use Pair/Share. Make Predictions and Interact in Think Aloud and Peer Tutoring. Use Collaborative Groups or Whole Class Discussions. Use (GO) for Themes, Vocabulary, Brainstorming, and Essays.

Use Concept Mapping, Frayer Model and Word Map forVocabulary. Engage in Deductive/Inductive Reasoning, and Hypothesis.

Kinesthetic: Students move through space (**Multi-Media Presentations**).

Complete Group Projects: Mime, Reader's Theater, Dance, Physical Games. Do Interviews. Write and Film a Book Commercial or Movie Trailer. Stage Oral Presentations. Make CDs. Use Internet.

Logical/Mathematical: Students quantify their instruction (**Literary Criticism**).

Use Critical Thinking Skills: Analytical, Synthesis, and Evaluative. Extrapolate in Socratic Seminar for Critical Thinking.

Research "The Secret of Prisoner No. 445," and the Holocaust. Research The Terrafugia Sport Aircraft.

Make Social, Philosophical, Economical, Psychological, Physiological and Political Connections.

Design Games: "Jeopardy" or "Who Wants To Be A Millionaire?" Recognize Propaganda Techniques and Faulty Logic.

Debate reasons why you believe getting an education in America is/or is not a bigger issue today than it was ten years ago.

Interview or do a profile or conduct a case study on an octogenarian. Get his/her ideas about our bodies not being ours. Find out their views on being older and how their relatives treat them.

Intrapersonal: Students connect to their personal life or worldview (**LA**).

Engage in Reflection, Silent Reading, Reading Logs and Journals. Design Self-evaluations, and Use Self-made Multimedia Reports. Use Computer Technology (Tutorial and Program Learning).

Musical: Students express themselves using rhythms and melody (**Oral Responses To Literary**).

Write and Sing a Song. Create Music with an Instrument.

Rap Vocabulary Words or Sing Five Words at a Time in the Melody of an Opera. Write and Recite Poetry.

Existentialist: Students make connections to philosophical issues and mankind's relationship to the universe **(Oral/Silent Communications).**

Devote Time for Spiritual Growth. Make Good Choices.

Recognize Better Alternatives. Learn to Visualize. Listen to Classical or Jazz Music. Read Self-Help Books. Engage in Exercising. Spend Time Alone. Escape Introspectively—Meditate.

Naturalist: Students appreciate nature **(Oral/Silent Communications).**

Do Nature Walks. Visit the Zoo. Have a Pet. Plant: Trees, Flowers, Fruits, and Vegetables. Be Concern for Eco-Systems.

Support an Animal or Global Organization for Life or Hunger. Classify and Categorize Activities, and Travel.

How many of you have pets and appreciate their companionship? Would you consider supporting a global organization for medical research or hunger?

What if you had your own aviary? What birds would you have?

Evaluations: Use a variety of assessments.

Use Teacher and Student Rubrics, Checklists, Portfolios, Tests, Projects, Anecdotal Notes, Journals, Quizzes, and the Essay Process.

Homework: Lessons completed outside the classroom are the teacher's choice based on the teaching methodologies used for differentiating learning in the classroom.

Vocabulary

Use appropriate vocabulary strategies for the students as long as the
activity aligns with specific standards and objectives of the lesson.

ad infinitum
articulated
averred
cerebrated
chattels
collaborated
convictions
culminating
definitive
explicated
iconography
infractions
kudos
mahogany
miscreants
nincompoop
opposition
predisposition
preposterous
serrated
sonata
subjective

Word Wall

Draw a medium, black silhouette of a jaguar.
Cut it out and place on wall.
Use a red marker and write vocabulary words on sentence strips.
Cut off excess ends.
Display words around silhouette.

If the word wall were used as a bulletin board, the title would read:

In the Zone of Changes with a few themes being displayed:
courage, determination, strength, love, friendship.

Whole Class/Pair Share Discussion

Look for the author's use of literary devices. Select one example from the text for each listed below. Include the page numbers. Then discuss your discoveries, their meanings/suggestions, and the impressions you acquired during your reading about the characters, events or situations.

Figures of speech

Simile:

Metaphor:

Personification:

Alliteration:

Hyperbole:

Oxymoron:

Other Literary Devices To Look For

Anecdote:

Symbolism:

Allusion:

Imagery:

Flashback:

Onomatopoeia:

Stream of Consciousness:

Foreshadowing:

S ... Words Related To The Characters

On page 76, Brenda's Saturday morning run is shaped like an S. In groups, brainstorm and list 15-20 words beginning with the letter S from the text. Discuss the symbolic meaning of the alphabet by selecting 7 or more words to describe a character of your choice. Use appropriate quotes from the text (include page numbers) to support your explication, interpretations, and analysis. If this exercise is used for writing a descriptive paragraph or an essay, please follow the rules for Standard English and use sentence variety.

Nexus

Page:
Paragraph:

Make a connection to your life and compare it to one of the situations or problems in the story. Answer all statements or questions in complete sentences.

Summarize the situation or problem in the story that relates to your life.

State and compare your situation or problem that you have encountered or lived through during your life.

Reflect on your situation or problem. Briefly discuss your thoughts that lead to your actions, not your reactions.

Introspection: Explain what you would do differently based on your actions if you had to experience the same situation or problem again.

Reflections

Title:
Author:

List the specific learning activities that you enjoyed. Then complete each sentence starter in a complete sentence. Use Standard English and punctuate correctly.

I discovered . . . .

I learned . . . .

I thought . . . .

List the specific learning activities that you did not enjoy.

I suggest that . . . .

I wonder (why, what, how) . . . .

Optional: Write a reflective essay using the writing process appropriate for grade level. Include the following: brainstorming activity, outline, first draft and rewrites with references to the text with quotations, and page numbers.

Notes

Frayer, Fredrick. Frayer Model: *http://homepage.mac.com/johnevers/medi.*

Gerberi, Danielle and Herman, Deirdre, Et al., eds. *Health Solutions for Managing Stress.* Rochester, Minnesota: Mayo Foundation Medical Education and Research, 2005.

Gradner, Howard. *Multiple Intelligences: The Theory in Practice.* New York: Basic, 1993.

Holy Bible, (The Old and New Testament) in the King James Version.

Tennessee: Thomas N. Publishers, Inc., 1984.

Kafka, Franz. *The Metamorphosis.* New York: A Bantam Classic, 1986.

Kaiser Permanente, "Stress Management, Mind/Body," SCPMG Regional Health Education, 2004, www.kaiserpermanente.org.

McCann, Hugh W. "The Secret of Prisoner No. 44451."

American Visions. July 1986: 37-41.

"Miranda Warning," *Wikipedia Encyclopedia.* Wikipedia Foundation, n.d., Web 25, Mar. 2010.

Terrafugia. The Transition, a Roadable Light Sport Aircraft, *www. Terrafugia.com.*

Thompkins, Gail E. 50 *Literacy Strategies Step-By-Step,* New Jersey: Prentice-Hall, Inc., 1998.

Wright, Ellen and Calfee, Bob, Et al., English-Language Arts-Kindergarten Through Grade Twelve Content Standards for California Public Schools, "Grades Eleven and Twelve." Sacramento, CA: California Department of Education Press, 1998.

www.readingquest.org—Vocabulary Word Map.

About the Author

Thank You

Thank You teaches children or anyone else how to express gratitude in over twenty-five different languages. Each page emanates with synchronized images and words that are classic, varied, and the essence of living and articulating thank you daily. Cleveland has written a book fit for anyone's coffee table or shelf or for a quick read and especially fit for anyone who enjoys expressing gratitude and acknowledging one's kindness.

Water Colored Soul

Water Colored Soul, a poetry collection, expresses how the poet has pulled back the leaves on this genre to expose a freshness that will transcend generations and her svelte lines rivet with excitement. Divided into three sections, the collection deals with accepting and rejecting love, visualizing images of people, and provoking thought about social issues in our society.

Love, a butterfly, flutters in quickly.
When it's time to part, love drags away like a 300 pound cotton sack.